A Flight Home

by

Richard Jones

Bloomington, IN Milton Keynes, UK

authorHOUSE

AuthorHouse™
1663 Liberty Drive, Suite 200
Bloomington, IN 47403
www.authorhouse.com
Phone: 1-800-839-8640

AuthorHouse™ UK Ltd.
500 Avebury Boulevard
Central Milton Keynes, MK9 2BE
www.authorhouse.co.uk
Phone: 08001974150

First published by AuthorHouse 8/22/2006

ISBN: 1-4259-4253-9 (sc)

Printed in the United States of America
Bloomington, Indiana

This book is printed on acid-free paper.

DEDICATION

To my dear wife Meg, Myrnie Allan, Janet Howells and our friends
Ken and Dee Ivison who helped with this book.

PROLOGUE

'There isn't any more. I've given you more than I dare already,' the man said lifting his head off the pillow.

'You were told that this was your last warning,' Raul replied. 'Either you write the cheque now or that's it. Those are my instructions.'

'Raul, he's disappeared. If I could only make contact there wouldn't be a problem, but I have to speak to him first.'

'That's not good enough my friend,' Raul said. 'It's today or finito. You know the score.'

'I know, I know,' the man said getting out of the bed. 'Raul I beg of you, just a few more days.'

The man, who was naked, except for a blue and white polka dot cravat, began to walk out of the bedroom. He was halfway to the door, then turned around.

'It's no good. I refuse to do it. You'll have to wait.'

Raul knew then what he had to do. It was his living, his contract. If he didn't comply, they'd do the same to him.

The man was now moving towards the bathroom. Raul got out of the bed and followed, slipping his large hands over the man's shoulders, just as he'd done so many times before, caressing with a lover's affection. He slid them around the man's neck and fingered the cravat.

'Good-bye my sweet friend,' Raul said. 'You've been good to me.'

Slowly, and tenderly at first, he pulled the two ends of the cravat in opposite directions. Then tighter and tighter, with the strength of his forearms, until the man's eyes bulged. The knot tightened, the skin became taut, their naked bodies were touching, close and warm as they had been in bed. The man struggled, but his tiny frame was no match for Raul's muscular strength.

'No Raul,' the man gasped, choking.

Desperately he tried to free himself. He hooked his leg behind Raul's and twisted. They tumbled. As they fell Raul spotted the bronze figurine. His hand grabbed out for it and as they hit the ground he violently smashed it into the side of the man's head.

CHAPTER

JENNY MILLINGTON WAS SITTING IN HER NEW SOLO FLAT IN ACTON, West London, flipping through the pages on her laptop.

Three hectic months had elapsed since taking up her post as Assistant Editor in the fiction department of Knott and Pearson, worldwide publishers, at their London office off Ealing Broadway. Aged twenty-six with an honours degree in English at Cambridge, publishing had seemed like a suitable career. Taking a year off to backpack through Europe with a friend helped formulate the decision. Alone in her small room, with fresh paint still permeating the air, she was wondering if she'd made the right choice.

That afternoon a three hour meeting with her editor, Imogen Quaith and the Financial Director, Frank Swan, had compounded the doubts. Swan, a short, dark, dapper little man with a pencil slim moustache, possessed a one track philosophy on profit margins. His summary was succinct; 'Your sales figures are just not good enough,' he stated. It was the early nineties and the end of the net book agreement had torn publishing in half.

'The house will be unable to carry its overheads much longer on the current turnover,' he continued to lecture. 'If things don't improve budgets will have to be slashed and redundancies considered.'

At home, afterwards, a headache meant relaxation was out of the question. So she made some toast, brewed a large pot of tea, kicked off the high heels that had pinched like hell all day and switched on the laptop.

To begin with her job had been fascinating and fun. Dealing with new authors was stimulating, their work enlightening, but with the finance people she felt out of her depth. Talking about budgets and job losses was scary. The hundred per cent mortgage on the flat was already straining her own domestic budget to its absolute limit.

Keying back over the sales figures for the last two years she could see Swan was right. She used to think most of their titles as nice little earners, but they'd all definitely taken a nosedive. Going back to the menu, she then went over it author by author, the answer was staring at her in the face. Two years ago 'Flame in the Sky' was at its peak. Casper Watkins' political novel had been mammoth.

While guiding the mouse to his file she couldn't recall his face, they hadn't met. Her eyes widened when the file came on screen. His birthplace, Dyserth, North Wales was just a few miles down the road from her home in nearby Ruthin. The three books before 'Flame in the Sky' sold reasonably well, but 'Sky' hit the jackpot all over the world. The royalties were immense. It was still selling, but there had been nothing since. She noticed three years had passed since he wrote it; 'What's the matter with these people back at the office,' she thought. To her, the answer to their problems seemed simple; Watkins needed coaxing back into life.

Satisfied she could face the following day, she folded up the laptop. In the fridge was a bottle of dry Martini, she added some ice, a slice of lemon, and a good measure of gin, then decided to ring home. Her mother answered.

'Jennifer my dear, how lovely to hear from you. Your father and I do wish you would ring more often.'

'Well I'm ringing now. Are you both well?'

'Your father's got his aches but we're making do. You know how he is.'

'Is he there mum? I just want to ask him something.'

Arthur Millington had been the headmaster at the local infants school. At some time during the fifties and sixties every child in the district had passed through his tutorship.

'You always ring when there's football on,' he said when he came to the phone.

'Hi Dad. I won't keep you long. Dad, did you teach a John Casper Watkins? He's a writer now and lives in London.'

'Oh Jenny there have been so many. John Casper Watkins?' she could almost hear him thinking. 'Yes, yes, they lived at Gwernaffield. Bright lad. There had been something funny in the family during the war. They tried to keep it quiet but you know what it's like around here. He went on to University I think. Why do you ask?'

'It's nothing important. He's one of our authors. You can go back to your football now. I may be up at the weekend. Tell me anything you remember then. Love you both.'

Jenny was slightly in awe of her Editor, Imogen Quaith. The woman once worked for the Express and, according to Imogen, she knew all the authors going back over twenty years, some intimately. But this idea had been burning in Jenny's brain all night and so it was with just a little trepidation that she knocked on her office door next morning.

'Oh, hi Jenny. Come in,' Imogen said. 'Hope you're not too shell shocked after yesterday,' she snorted. 'Frank Swan can be a bit of a bastard, but he's only doing his job.'

'The pocket battleship' was how some of the lads in the office referred to Imogen. Short and stocky with close cropped red hair, she always managed a well tailored appearance. A lilac two piece suit with a long-line structured jacket, over a mandarin blouse was that days offering. Rings accompanied most of her stubby fingers. She smoked constantly and possessed a fearsome temper. Jenny smiled and tried to compose herself.

'Well that's what I wanted to see you about,' she said.

Imogen had been reading a document. Slowly she lifted her eyes, removed her glasses and sighed, her standard response to being interrupted. Jenny continued.

'To see if we could improve things I spent last night looking through the lap-top files.'

'My God, it's nice to know we have someone conscientious here for a change,' Imogen replied with a heavy hint of sarcasm. 'Well go on, what did the magic screen reveal?'

3

Jenny coughed to clear her throat.

'What's happened to Casper Watkins?' she asked. 'Surely a new book from him would
revitalise our figures?'

Imogen set her glasses down amongst the clutter on the desk, took a cigarette from a packet in her handbag, inserted it into a long brown cigarette holder, before easing back in her chair.

'Well that's a very good question,' she said while lighting the cigarette. 'That man has just disappeared off the face of this earth. Even the chairman, Lord Rathenberg, has been involved. He's given his son, Anthony, the task of finding him. Watkins could name his own advance, but as far as I am aware we've had no luck.'

'Could he be dead?' Jenny asked.

'Not according to his agent. But he doesn't say much that's helpful.'

'I have an idea,' Jenny said, with a degree of uncertainty.

Imogen looked at her with questioning eyes and took a long draw on the cigarette.

'My dear Jenny, for the past three months Anthony Rathenberg has employed a firm of private detectives to try and trace him. Last month we stopped paying his royalties. How do you think you could succeed when all that's failed?'

Jenny coughed nervously.

'Well I wasn't going to tell you this, but before coming to see you I sneaked into publicity. I know I am not supposed to, but I've had a look at his file.' A frown had formed on Imogens' face. Jenny kept going before she was shot down.

'It's all in a good cause, isn't it,' Jenny said quickly. 'You see when I first looked at the figures I thought we were dealing with some swish London author. I mean there's the posh apartment in Ebury Terrace, the well publicised affair with Caroline Di Angello. The trips to New York and Hollywood. The photographs with her in the Bahamas. It all seemed to point to a man who enjoyed the glamorous Bohemian life.' Jenny paused for breath, then added a smile to quell Imogen's frown.

'Go on,' Imogen said and sucked on her cigarette.

'Well, then I spotted something that made me think again. You see Imogen, he's Welsh, like me.'

Imogen's frown was getting deeper.

'He was born in Dyserth. His mother's home is Gwernaffield, that's about ten miles down the road from where I lived.'

'So what!!'

'Imogen, if a man from around there wanted to go to ground he wouldn't do it in any of the places your detectives may have looked. I know that part of the world. Deep down he's a country boy and just like a fox, he'd know how to hide from the pack.'

'But we've checked around his mother's home, he's not there.'

'No! That would be too simple. But there may be a clue there. The local people wouldn't open up to a London firm of detectives.' Jenny began waving her arms in concert with her words. 'You see the Welsh aren't all that impressed by glamour and fame. If it comes their way they'll take it, but it's not that important.'

Imogen looked bewildered.

'Well, what have you got in mind?' she said knocking the ash off her cigarette. 'I can't afford to let you have time off to go gadding about Wales, looking for this man. We've got books to publish here, not to mention Frank Swan breathing down our necks.'

'I wouldn't expect that but I could spend my weekends on it. I have to go up there to see my family. If you would just give me clearance to enquire on the firm's behalf, that's all I am asking.'

'Jenny I don't know. I'll have to speak to Anthony Rathenberg. It's his responsibility. This could be dangerous. Casper may be in all sorts of trouble we don't know about.'

'I've hitchhiked through Turkey,' Jenny said. 'North Wales wouldn't be as dangerous as that.'

'Well you'll have to leave it with me,' Imogen retorted curtly. She stubbed out her cigarette and replaced her glasses. 'Now we really must get on with publishing some books.'

Later in the day Imogen buzzed through on the internal phone, wanting to see her. Jenny was in the middle of proof checking. She dashed across the office.

'Oh Jenny there you are,' Imogen said. 'I don't think you've met Anthony Rathenberg?'

Jenny froze in the doorway. Standing alongside Imogen's desk was the most delicious looking fair haired man. Very tall, probably in his late thirties, with flecks of grey at the temples, all she could do was stare.

'This is Jenny Millington, who I was telling you about,' Imogen continued.

'How very pleasant to make your acquaintance Miss Millington,' Rathenberg said. The words rolled effortlessly off his tongue. 'Imogen's been telling me about your interest in our truant author. How do you feel you can help?'

Having just finished a biscuit she prayed there weren't crumbs left showing. When she looked up, the hue of his blue eyes, the cut of his sharp jaw line, his whole demeanour, caused her words to stumble.

'Well, er. I just feel that I have er, a closer knowledge of the area he was brought up in, a-an-and the character of the people from around there,' she stuttered. Her every word sounded inept, her every syllable inadequate. She coughed to cover her embarrassment and tried once more, this time without looking at Anthony Rathenberg.

'What I am trying to say, is that you have only known this man as a successful author on the London scene. But for the early part of his life he lived in a close knit agricultural community. If he's really under pressure his mind will relocate in those terms. If he doesn't want to be found, a London private eye isn't going to know where to look.' She paused and glanced up. They were both staring at her. 'What I'd like to do is to go back to his roots, and try and piece together the reasons for his disappearance.'

Anthony Rathenberg was smiling. There was a moment, just for a few seconds, when Jenny regretted ever having mentioned the subject. Standing in front of them both, in Imogen's office, she felt silly, like a schoolgirl up before the headmaster.

'Perhaps it might be best if you talk to his agent first,' Rathenberg said. 'Maybe Imogen can arrange for you to see Henson Littlewood. With your pretty face he may reveal something he hasn't told us. You will have to be careful though, he and Casper are very close.'

Jenny still felt embarrassed.

'If you come up with anything positive perhaps you can let me know,' Rathenberg continued. 'But I don't want you wasting too much of the firm's time on this. If Casper doesn't want to write books there are plenty of people who do.'

When he left the room Jenny had to lean on the edge of Imogen's desk. Her knees had begun to tremble.

'OK, let's see what you can come up with,' Imogen said. 'But you heard Anthony. I don't want you wasting time on this.'

'Imogen I do think you are a rat.'

Imogen looked as though she was about to cut loose.

'For not warning me about our dishy Managing Director, I mean.' Jenny added quickly.

Imogen smiled.

'Don't get any big ideas. He's spoken for and she's very wealthy. Just be careful Jenny.'

That evening after eating, Jenny settled on her divan. Imogen had authorised for her to borrow Casper's file. She kicked off her sneakers, stretched out her legs and noticed her toenails needed painting.

There was a lot to digest. Many disputes, mainly about royalties. Some of the more virulent arguments centred on the firm's attempts to alter his text. It all pointed to a fiery Welsh temperament, just what she'd expected.

His biographical notes indicated a fairly mediocre academic life. Denbigh grammar school, then an arts degree at Liverpool University. Afterwards he became a hack reporter. Firstly for the Rhyl Journal and later on for the Liverpool Evening Post. He was in his early thirties before he produced his first novel. A descriptive tale about life in the classy areas of the Wirral. It sold moderately well but certainly didn't place him amongst the best sellers. Two successful political thrillers followed. They established his reputation. Then he moved to London to team up with his long standing friend and agent Henson Littlewood. It seems they were at University together.

According to the office wags there was some doubt about Henson's sexual persuasion but there could be no confusion over Casper's. Press cuttings revealed a string of well known female liaisons. The synopsis of his first novel epitomised the lurid life of a journalist. She made a note of his titles and would start reading them next day.

Caroline Di Angello came on the scene when he was writing 'A Flame in the Sky'. One of the faces of the early nineties, she found fame as a television actress with a raunchy part in a 'soap'. That led to films, Hollywood and two major box office extravaganzas. Their well documented relationship lasted about three years. For a time she moved into his Ebury Terrace apartment, then their relationship floundered.

A group of publicity photographs fell out of the file. Some of Casper by himself and a couple with Caroline Di Angello the house had used to launch 'Sky'. Together they made a glamorous couple. Caroline's curly blonde hair, high cheekbones and sylph like figure regularly enlivened the tabloid pages on many a dull news day. Casper's features were more rugged. Tall, dark haired and muscular. Jenny wouldn't really call him handsome, manly and forceful was a description that came into her head. It was very late when she put the file down. She made a note of his mother's address; the detectives report revealed Caroline Di Angello's ex-directory number.

Sleep that night came quickly. The faces of Casper and Caroline Di Angello featured in her dreams, like an old movie she had seen a long time ago, but couldn't remember the title or the story.

CHAPTER

HE JUMPED FROM THE COASTAL PATH DOWN ONTO THE BEACH. THE sudden movement startled the oystercatchers; they took off in formation. A lone heron stood motionless on the pinnacle of a small rock, while a pair of cormorants energetically flapped their wings on a limpet covered slab.

It was eight thirty in the morning, the tide had just turned and he could walk the rest of the way to the village across the bay. The sharpness of the wind bit at his cheeks. Flecks of spray flew along the virgin sand. The peak of a white baseball cap half covered his face; two days growth of beard disguised the rest. A red anorak over a polo neck pullover kept out the wind; his wellingtons made deep imprints in the sand.

The shop behind the harbour wall braved all the elements. A plethora of advertising signs covered the frontage, most of them out of date. Cautiously he peered in through a salt-sprayed window. A fluttery bell pinged above his head when he pushed the door open.

'Ah, there you are now John,' he heard a voice say when he was inside. 'And how are you today?'

In the dim light his eyes strained to find her. Merchandise pressed in on all sides, shelves stacked to ceiling height compounded the gloom.

'I'm fine Katherine,' he replied spotting her movement. 'How about you?'

'Oh, all right I guess. The boiler blew out in the night. This wind gets me down some days.'

He could see her properly now. Brown hair, shaped around her face, green eyes, bright like diamonds, skin smooth like cream.

'Do you want me to look at it?' he asked.

'No, I've fixed it. See if you can do something about the wind though.'

He smiled.

Katherine Walker was the sole owner of the shop since her husband died. They'd both left secure jobs in the Midlands for this wild and rocky shore. An ideal about running a village store, cum post office had filled their heads. Then Ken was killed in a road crash, three years last May. Now there was just the shop and two young children, Paul nine, Sarah seven. At thirty-six that was hard going.

'Have you any of those frozen chicken pies left?' he asked. 'The one I had last week was very good.'

'I may have. If you'd let me cook you dinner I could make something much nicer.'

'I'll manage fine, honestly Katherine,' he replied.

Three years of struggle had taken its toll on Katherine Walker. Being a widow was tough. Wild fluctuations in seasonal trade hadn't helped. Two wet summers had been cruel, but living a hundred and fifty miles from friends and family was what made it hard. The lines on her face were a testimony to her struggle. The glow in her eyes though, when she looked at John, indicated she was not about to give up.

'Oh well please yourself then,' she said and bent into the freezer for the chicken pie. A tight fitting blue tracksuit accentuated her curves. Watching, he was forced to look away and took a newspaper from the rack. Deliberately she brushed against him when she moved to the till.

'That will be two pounds fifty please,' she said. 'Will I be seeing you tonight?' she added.

'About ten, if that's all right,' he replied, placing the money on the counter. He would never visit when the children were up.

'Are you sure you can spare the time?' she said. It was a subject on which they agreed to differ.

'See you later then,' he said moving towards the door. He knew she'd be watching. Feeling nervous, he struggled with the catch. Torrential rain and endless gales battered those westerly shores. Woodwork takes a long time to dry out. The door stuck and he had to tug it open.

The beach was his preferred route to and from the village. There was a track from the road but to use it advertised his occupancy. Reunited with the sand he began to stride out. Last night, half a bottle of whisky induced a cramped sleep. By the time he reached the rocky outcrop behind his home, the stiffness was just about gone.

The small cottage he lived in was built of local stone. There was a corrugated roof. Four tiny windows let in the light, two at the front and two at the back. He removed his boots and tiptoed across a flagstone floor. One room encompassed the living arrangements, with the exception of a cold damp bathroom extension at the rear. A precarious wooden staircase led to a bedroom in the roof, with a skylight. Through it, if he stood on his bed, was a view of the sea and the impending westerly storms.

The smouldering embers of last night's fire puttered in the hearth. He threw on a limb of ash, slumped into the only armchair and watched an array of sparks fly up the chimney.

CHAPTER

HENSON LITTLEWOOD LIVED IN A LARGE THREE STOREY, VICTORIAN terraced house in Kensington. When Jenny phoned he sounded rather quaint. Phrases ending in 'Yes, yes, my dear,' and 'of course my dear; anything to help, my dear,' liberally filled out his vocabulary.

They agreed to meet after work at his house. She was nervous when she pressed on the bell; a small brass plate above it proclaimed 'Henson Littlewood - Literary Agent'. His metallic voice in the intercom made her jump. She giggled her name in response. 'Yes, yes, my dear. Turn the handle and come in,' he said.

The big square hall was panelled in oak. Palms and bay trees decorated the entrance. Classical paintings adorned the walls. It was serene, cool and elegant. Her high heels echoed on the marble tiles and she heard him call down from above.

'Ah there you are Miss Millington. Please come up, come up.' He was looking down at her from the top step of an exquisitely carved wooden staircase. Her knees trembled as she ascended.

'Sorry to drag you up here my dear, but it's so stuffy down there in my old office. My, you are pretty aren't you. Casper would like you.' The day before she had added some highlights to her short blonde hair and she was wearing her best black suit.

A small hand stretched out to aid her up the final step. The touch was light, effeminate. His wizened face had delicate rabbit-like features, making his age difficult to judge. Certainly over fifty; maybe even sixty she thought. About five four in height, with straight brown hair, he wore a beige cardigan over a check shirt, a flowery cravat and corduroy trousers. Straightaway they agreed on first name terms.

He led the way to a spacious first floor lounge with heavy brocade wallpaper, dark furniture and more avant garde paintings.

'Oh what a lovely room,' she said.

'It's my favourite. The light up here is very good. Will you take some tea my dear?' he asked and gestured to a high backed chair by an open window.

'That's kind of you. Yes please,' she said and sat down. When she looked around, he was behind her, pouring tea from a silver tea pot. They exchanged more pleasantries while he fussed with her cup, before she got to the point.

'Henson, do you have any idea what might have happened to Casper? I mean it's so odd for a man at the height of his fame to just walk off the island.'

'Unfortunately not my dear. It's a mystery to me as well. I can't think why he's vanished or even where he may be.'

'Has he made any contact in the last few months?'

'No my dear. The last time I saw him he was sitting in the chair you are now in.' She watched him lift two scones off a silver service with a pair of silver tongs and delicately place them on a bone china plate, which he put on a small table alongside her.

'Was he unhappy?' Jenny asked.

'What's happy?' He shrugged and sat in a chair opposite her with his tea. 'He looked as well as I've seen him look in a long time.'

'Has anybody been to his apartment?'

'Yes, I have a key and call regularly. I deal with his mail and business matters. It's something I've done for years anyway.' He supped at his tea, slurping the last gulp. 'He's not very good at that sort of thing and usually leaves it all to me.'

Jenny bit into the scone. It was light like air, she hadn't tasted one as good for years.

'Henson these are delicious.'

'I made them myself. One of my little hobbies.'

'You must give me the recipe. Do you think he's still alive?' she continued.

'I'm convinced of that, my dear. You see his bank statement stopped going to his home. I deal with his business account, which takes care of the apartment and his writing. I'm a signatory on that but his own personal bank statement is going somewhere else.'

'Surely the bank will give you the address, you're his agent?'

'It seems they have strict instructions on that. I have written, care of them, but there's been no reply.'

Jenny had to tread carefully. Anthony Rathenberg had said he and Casper were very close and she didn't want to overstep the mark.

'According to my information his mother's still alive?' Jenny said. 'Does she know he's missing?'

'Sort of.' Henson replied, looking vague. 'Trouble is she's in her eighties and gets confused. You see he's lived away for so long. When I tell her he's not around, I don't really think she understands. He was always gadding off somewhere, on some jaunt, and I don't want to worry her unduly.' He shook his head from side to side and smiled. 'Years ago he used to bring her to London. Take her to the Savoy. Embarrass her to death with all his highfalutin friends. John always makes me laugh she used to say, but that was a long time ago,' he shook his head again.

'Henson can I ask a favour?' she paused for a second and took a deep breath. 'When you next visit the apartment, could I possibly come with you? Not to nose or pry, I just want to get a feel of things.'

He smiled, a crooked smile, which contorted his face into funny angles. Jenny continued.

'You see when I began delving into all this I discovered he was brought up near my home in North Wales. I believe a clue might come from there, but I have to see how much he's changed.'

At first she thought he was going to refuse, then his face lit up and all the awkward angles dissolved.

'I thought there was something similar about you,' he said. 'I noticed it when you came up the stairs. You have the same glint in your eye, the same lilt in your voice, you're much prettier of course,' he chuckled and she blushed. 'I was planning to visit the apartment on Thursday. You're welcome to come along if you think it will help.'

'You are an angel, but you're going to embarrass me to death if you continue to say how pretty I am.'

'That's my intention my dear.'

A small silver clock on the mantelpiece chimed six, a miniature silver eagle sitting alongside, caught her eye. Around the room there were many trinkets, most of them silver. Nearly all the tops featured objet d'art. An epicurean is Henson, she thought.

'What about Caroline Di Angello?' she asked. 'I understand they split up. Would that have caused him to disappear?'

'No, that all finished a long time ago,' he replied and made a funny puckering motion with his lips. 'At the beginning it was very physical. You couldn't keep them apart. But the intensity went out of it and in the end they began to rile each other. I think he was glad when it was over.'

Their conversation drifted into anecdotes about Casper's life. When the clock chimed for the half hour she made her excuses to leave.

'I'll need to check with my filofax for Thursday,' he said. 'It's downstairs in the study.'

A room off the hall, by the front door led to his office. Small and square with book lined walls from floor to ceiling, a bay window, shaded with blinds on the outside wall, provided the only daylight. He fussed and fiddled amongst the clutter on the desk. The room was stuffy, a sweet pungent aroma tickled her nostrils. A deeper breath confirmed it was pot. A smell reminiscent from her student days.

'Everything to hand if only I could put a hand on it,' Henson said, still delving. 'I was using the damn thing this afternoon.'

Manuscripts covered the desk and the tables around it. Most of them were open at haphazard angles, some with the corner of the page turned down, as though he had been interrupted and intended to go back when time allowed.

'Ah here we are,' he said holding up the filofax. 'Twelve o'clock should be fine. I have a meeting at ten, but I should be free by then.'

She made for the front door.

'I hope you'll come and see me again,' he said on her way out.

Jenny liked Henson, although her mind swam with conjecture on the way home. All the time she'd been there, his face bore a contrived look of acquiescence and she couldn't decide if it was for her benefit, or if he knew more than he was saying?

15

That evening Jenny sat at the window of her flat, watching the big jets floating into Heathrow. Compared to Henson's elegant residence, with all its adornments, her tiny room looked bare and desolate. A weekend there didn't appeal much, so she decided to travel North, after work on Friday. She rang home.

'Mum I was hoping to come up at the weekend,' she said when her mother answered. 'Is there a spare bed for me or are the tartan army coming?' The tartan army was her collective term for her sister Isabel's tribe. Partly because there were so many of them, five in all, partly because they created so much noise, and partly because Isabel's husband, Duncan, was Scottish. He was an orthopaedic surgeon at Glasgow Royal Infirmary. Being Scottish was all right, but unfortunately Duncan was Scottish in the worst kind of way. He constantly romanced about the 'misty lochs and bonny hills' and on festive occasions he would always wear a kilt. Jenny thought it was all a bit banal for a man who was brought up in East Kilbride and openly bragged about voting Tory.

'Of course there is a bed for you my dear,' her mother said. 'You can have your old room. Your father will be so pleased. I'll go and tell him now.'

'Don't disturb him Mum, it's his tele time, he'll only curse if he misses something. If the other lot turn up, where will they all sleep?'

'They can sleep together and those that can't, can go on the sofa. Of course you must have your old room. It'll be wonderful for us all to be together again. Your father will like that.'

'No Mum he won't. If we all turn up he'll look tight lipped and go into the greenhouse for a bit of peace and quiet, just like he always does.'

'How's your job going?' Mother asked.

'I'll tell you about work when I see you. That's part of the reason for coming.'

'Oh dear. Everything's all right, is it? You know how impetuous you are.'

'Yes mother, everything's fine. I'll save all my impetuosity for Isabel and the children.'

'Oh you two are funny.'

CHAPTER

NIGHT TIME EVOKES SO MUCH THE DAYLIGHT SHUNS. AN OWL HOOTS in a distant tree. A fox lopes from a sand dune, looks left, then right and continues on. Breakers echo off the harbour wall, the silence draws attention to their roar.

Raucous laughter, mixed with muffled sounds of conversation, drift out of the Ship Inn. He hurries by, with collar up and cap down. Enshrined in a Norman tower, the church clock chimes ten. The alleyway behind the shop is dark like ink; his leg jars on the pedal of a bike. Cursing he feels for the door. Three knocks and wait, then another two; it's their agreed signal. A scrabble of hands on the other side, then he hears the bolt slide across.

'Are you all right?' he whispers.

'I suppose so,' is her hushed reply.

Darkness engulfs the kitchen. Now it's all familiar touch and feel. Inside her gown there's warm supple flesh. He comes alive, but there's still a maze of doors and passageways to negotiate. The haven of her bedroom is a long way away.

'I thought you'd know the way by now,' she chides as she quietly guides him through.

It's midnight when he tramps back across the bay. The moon is up, the roller coaster waves are a long way off. A folk tune he used to sing in school floods into his head. He mouths the words as he strides along. He is content on this rocky windswept shore.

CHAPTER

A MENTAL IMAGE OF CASPER WAS BEGINNING TO FORM IN JENNY'S mind. Reading his books helped. Devouring page after page at every opportunity, she couldn't believe their freshness. 'The Other Way' was written fifteen years back, but the characters literally jumped out of the text, as though they lived next door.

Casper definitely had talent, it was evident even then. Hurtling through the chapters she began to worry about her tack on this investigation. London life was totally different from anything up North, even she had discovered that. Maybe Casper had changed more than she thought. Perhaps her theory on this was wrong.

Her dilemma forced her to telephone Caroline Di Angello; something she had been dreading. The actress answered her call. A husky cultured voice embellished the pronunciation of her name.

'Miss Di Angello, I am sorry to trouble you. My name is Jenny Millington and I work for Casper Watkins's Publishers, Knott and Pearson,' she began. Her words were greeted with silence.

'We are trying to track him down,' she continued. She paused again, but her words still remained unanswered. 'A couple of new leads have come to light and I was wondering if I could see you to check them out?' Jenny lied and held her breath.

'That bastard can rot in hell as far as I am concerned,' Caroline Di Angello replied. The mask of culture had already slipped. An East End accent had crept into the rhetoric. 'He buggered off without saying a word. Anyway, I told those pricks from the detective agency everything I know. I don't want to go over it all again.'

Jenny coughed.

'Believe me Miss Di Angello I know how you must feel. He walked out on us as well. But my boss has lumbered me with the task of finding him. There's talk of a biography and I'm going to be out of a job if I don't come up with something on his whereabouts soon. It wouldn't be more than a few minutes, I promise.' Jenny was playing on the woman's vanity, hoping the possibility of a book and the publicity entailed would entice her to talk.

'I'm extremely busy at the moment. I'm off to Rome at the weekend, to shoot a new film with Claudio Karponti. You know, the gorgeous Italian hunk?' Jenny didn't know and she didn't really care, but she had to keep going.

'Oh how exciting. Perhaps I could see you before you go? I assure you it won't take long.'

There was a pause.

'The only day available is Wednesday. My beautician is coming here at twelve.'

'Could I possibly see you then?' Jenny cut in. 'I could come to your apartment. It is important to me, honestly.'

'Oh all right if you must. You can call at eleven forty five, but I don't give a fucking toss about that bloody Welshman. You won't be able to stay long, Justin's always on time.'

Jenny decided there and then that she didn't like Caroline Di Angello. The woman's every word stuck in her craw. A right little bitch was the phrase that came to mind.

That evening she finished reading Caspers' books. With each one the plots became more complicated, the settings more bizarre, but on every page the characters sparkled, like jewels in a crown.

Caroline Di Angello lived in a ritzy apartment block in Bloomsbury. A concrete and glass emporium, with coloured PVC. Jenny rang a door intercom, then waited a long time before Caroline answered.

A mirrored lift climbed eight floors to the penthouse, making a sucking noise as it rose. Standing at the door of her apartment Caroline looked everything Jenny had imagined. An enormous pair of sunglasses accentuated the high cheek bones. Her face was ghostly white, the lips glossy red, the blonde hair was tied back in a bun. A tall shapely figure was encased in a multi coloured shell suit.

'I can't spare long. I've started to put on my face, as you can see by all the cream,' Caroline said, touching her cheek. 'Justin will be here any minute.'

Jenny's attempt at a smile was wasted; Caroline had already moved inside, leaving Jenny to deal with the door.

'I'll try not to take too much of your time,' Jenny said, as she followed down a passage littered with art deco. 'As I mentioned on the phone, there's been this talk of a biography. With your long relationship I expect there'll be a chapter about you.'

They entered a spacious, garishly decorated living room. A wall of windows flooded in the sunlight. Caroline spun round to face her, pushed the sunglasses up into her hairline, and fixed her with a stare. Jenny was completely unprepared for the eyes. Their piercing blue set her back on her heels.

'You'll have to excuse the mess,' Caroline said, waving her arms about. Clothes were everywhere, on the table, on the chairs, on the floor. 'I just can't decide what to take to Italy. At this time of year you never know what the weather's going to be.' She cleared a small space amongst the jumpers and skirts and sat on the sofa, in the gap. Jenny was not offered a seat.

'It must be a problem,' Jenny replied. 'Caroline, when you last saw Casper did he seem unduly upset about anything?'

'Upset! Upset? I was the one who was upset. He promised to come up with the money, but he buggered off without saying a word. Upset, I'd make him upset if I found him.'

'What do you mean? Did he owe you money? You didn't mention that to the detectives.'

'No, well it was all under wraps at the time and Henson asked me to keep quiet about it. But I don't care anymore. I feel so let down about the whole thing. Casper can be at the bottom of the ocean as far as I'm concerned. You can put that in his biography.' She laughed, a harsh mocking sound, then continued. 'A quote from his former mistress. Put it on the inside flap. That'll stimulate sales!'

Jenny smiled.

'H'm. Well that sort of ties in with some of things I've discovered. I think Henson mentioned something about that. I'm meeting him at Casper's apartment tomorrow,' Jenny said and scratched her head. 'Caroline please can you tell me a bit more. My boss is on my back on this and so far I've really got nowhere.'

Caroline delved around under the clothes for her handbag and retrieved a packet of king sized American cigarettes and a marble cigarette lighter. She lit up a cigarette without offering one to Jenny, took a long deep draw and brushed back her hair with a sweep of her hand.

'Well it was all to do with a film we were going to make out of 'Flame in the Sky" Caroline began, while blowing smoke into the air. 'An American consortium was the lead group, but Casper was going to come up with some of the money as well. Because of his contract with you lot he didn't want anybody to know. That's why I never said anything before. He said the lawyers would sort it out when the time was right. I was going to star with another big name playing the political lead.'

'When was this?' Jenny asked.

The actress drew again on the cigarette and leant back in the settee.

'It all started when we were in New York, for the literary awards. We met up with these big swish movie types. You know, all stretch limousines and ponytails.' Jenny fluttered her eyes, trying not to interrupt. Caroline took another big draw on the cigarette, the ash had become an inch long.

'Anyway, after we got back some of their people came over for a meeting. We all met up at Casper's apartment. Henson was there as well. It was going to be so exciting.'

'What happened then?'

'Nothing. Casper just disappeared and left us all high and dry. I tell you the man's a louse. Personally I think he chickened out. Probably didn't have the money anyway.'

'Did he ever take you to North Wales?' Jenny asked. 'The trail I have seems to lead there.'

'Oh I don't know. Yes, I think we went there once, on our way back from Scotland. I can remember staying at some place called Llangollen or something like that. It was by a river. I remember that, but I was totally bored. I mean there was absolutely nothing to do. It was awful.'

'Did you meet any of his family? They live around there.'

'No, all I remember is being very bored. He left me on my own for an afternoon. Said he had to go and see somebody. It was late in the evening when he got back. He was in a foul mood. We had a row and came home the next day.'

'Was that before or after you went to America?'

'Oh a long time after that. We were still living together when we went to America, but I'd moved in here by then. We met the film people the day after we got back from North Wales. A few days after that Casper disappeared.'

The door buzzer sounded.

'That'll be Justin. I really must wind this up now. I've got so much to do.'

Jenny looked around while Caroline went to the door. The room was huge. The walls were painted canary yellow with blue dados. All the tables and cupboards were glass. It certainly didn't look comfortable. The clothes all had designer labels.

Justin was a tall muscular, macho looking young man with jet black, collar length hair and powerful eau de cologne. He wore a dark blue sleeveless vest and white slacks. His pearly white teeth dazzled like the fender on an American car when he smiled at Jenny.

'Justin, this is Jenny something or other from Casper's publishers and she's just leaving,' Caroline said.

'Hi,' he said and smiled again. The effect was startling.

'Good luck with your new film,' Jenny replied on her way out, not meaning a word of it.

In the tube station she bought a newspaper. As the train rattled back to Ealing, she came across a picture of Caroline Di Angello on the showbiz page. It was featured alongside a press release for a movie with Claudio Karponti. The article mentioned that filming in Italy was about to begin. It went on to say that finance for the movie was being provided by a consortium that included Karponti and Caroline Di Angello.

When Jenny showered on Thursday morning, her bio-rhythms conveyed that something awful was about to happen. There was a flutter in her chest and a tenseness in her forehead. She couldn't define it, but later on she remembered the feeling.

To begin with Imogen was particularly bitchy about her having time off to meet Henson at Casper's apartment. The dissent had carried over from yesterday's meeting with Caroline Di Angello.

'I thought all this Helen Mirren stuff was going to take place in your own time,' Imogen had scolded; deep furrows on her brow emphasised her annoyance.

'I'll only be gone for an hour and I'll work through my lunch hour to make up,' Jenny replied.

'You make sure you do,' Imogen retorted and took a long drag on her cigarette. 'I sometimes wonder if you people think we are running a bloody holiday camp here.'

Imogen's words were still ringing in her ears as she ran from the tube station to Ebury Terrace. She had intended to stroll and savour the ambience of the Georgian houses, but she was out of breath and puffing by the time she entered the lobby. It was ten past twelve, she was late. Casper's apartment was on the third floor. In the lift she felt her body shiver; perhaps she had a bout of flu, she thought.

The door to the apartment was open. For some strange reason her skin was melting like ice when she walked through.

'Henson I'm here,' she called out. A marble hallway, with statues and busts of the same material, lined the way to a pair of double doors. She pushed through. The room inside was enormous, big enough for tennis she thought.

'Henson, it's Jenny. Are you in?'

Her eyes widened in awe. Huge sash windows flooded light into a room, with a back wall of green tapestry and gilded mirrors. An elaborate satinwood and moulded plaster ceiling was highlighted in gold. The furniture was a mixture of Italian Renaissance and Louis X1V revival styles. The curtains were green silk velour and the centre of a vast Savonnerie carpet was also green. Under one of the front windows a mahogany hand carved table was littered with mail. At one end a gold arched lamp was switched on, alongside it a word processor was positioned.

There's something sacrosanct about a writer's desk she thought, as her fingers fluttered along it's surface. A silver paperknife bearing the initials 'C W' lay across a pile of recently opened envelopes. Some of the postmarks bore yesterday's date. Suddenly her spine shivered, as though a cold wind had numbed her back.

At the far end of the room, an open door led to an inner hall. She headed that way calling Henson's name, until a strange smell, a sickly sweetness, mixed with a rancid odour made her stop. Another collection of doors confronted her, one was open. The odour seemed to emanate from there. Inside was a large double bedroom. A veritable Casanova's lair, with more walled mirrors and a circular bed on a raised dais. The duvet was crumpled as though it had been slept in. The bedside table was askew, the lamp had been knocked over. A shaft of electric light edged out from a bathroom.

In the doorway she froze and screamed, a piercing scream that flew through the air like a knife. Blood stained water filled the bath and in it lay Henson's crumpled naked body. A hole in the side of his head oozed blood, a blue cravat was knotted around his throat, what she thought was hair had been a wig. Matted with blood, it was tilted ridiculously over one eye. Streaky red water dripped over the side of the bath. Smudged footprints covered the wet terrazzo floor tiles.

She had to look away. Look at anything except what confronted her. She began to shiver uncontrollably. The trembling turned into a pulsating shake, bile rose in her throat, her hands reached out for the basin and clung on while her stomach wretched.

Fear, panic, faint, everything became a blur, but somehow or another she rang the police. Before she had time to think they were swarming around her with flashlight cameras, plastic bags and loud voices. It was a nightmare. While they dealt with it all she sat at Casper's desk, staring out of the window, while her body still uncontrollably shook. A woman police officer, Julie, sat with her, made strong tea and dealt words of comfort.

What they did with Henson's body she didn't know and couldn't bear to turn round to find out. A feeling of numbness had replaced the shaking by the time a Detective Inspector John Palmer introduced himself. He told her he was in charge. Said they would require a statement 'at the station'. Tall and thin with dark receding hair, he spoke with a harsh cockney accent, while his hazel eyes flitted round the room.

At the police station they wanted her fingerprints and DNA. They tested her for drugs and took her photograph. In all it took over three hours. Then more waiting around, with Julie dispensing tea until Palmer reappeared. He was not so considerate. Words swaggered out of his mouth. What was she was doing in the apartment? How long had she known Henson? Why was she meeting him there? What was all this business about Casper disappearing? Where was his home in North Wales?

For half an hour they sat eyeball to eyeball across a table. When his vitriol paused she could see the blackheads on the side of his nose. 'Are you sure you're telling me the truth?' he questioned. By then a confused haze had replaced the numbness in her mind. 'Yes,' she yelled. He relented, lent back in his chair, scratched his hair, then was back at her again with his chin thrusting forward. 'When had anybody last seen Casper? What was his relationship with Henson? How long had they known each other? When had she begun working for Knott and Pearson? What did she do before that?'

In the end her head spun, she couldn't cope and broke down. Tears flooded her face. Palmer left the room. Julie returned to re-administer more tea.

Another man, Roberts, appeared to take her statement. 'We'll need to know where to contact you over the next few days,' he said when she had finished dictating.

'What the hell has that got to do with you?' she exploded.

'Miss, this is a murder enquiry.'

'I was planning to visit my parents in North Wales at the weekend,' she said, relenting.

'We'll need to know their address and telephone number,' he said. Her mother would have a fit she thought. 'And we'll have to retain your passport,' he added. 'Just a precaution you understand.'

'Surely you don't think I did this,' she ranted.

'It's routine procedure miss. We have to eliminate all the possibilities first.'

Why, oh why had she become involved. Her parents would be panic stricken, and the office, 'Oh my God I've forgotten to telephone the office.' Imogen would be paralytic, she'll think I've absconded. She looked at her watch. Five O'clock, 'Jesus Christ, I'm in for it now. I must ring my office. I was supposed to be back in a hour.'

'As you wish miss. Afterwards Julie will give you a lift home. If you could give her your passport, it would help.'

'I keep telling you, I arranged to meet Henson there to try and get some background on Casper Watkins. He's one of our authors and he's disappeared. Do you seriously think I shot Henson, lifted him into the bath, drowned him and after all that phoned you. If you think that, you're sick.'

A pained smile spread across Roberts' face.

'I am only doing my job miss.'

Phoning Imogen didn't help. 'More time wasted,' were her first words. No statement of sorrow about Henson's death. No platitudes of comfort for Jenny's predicament. Just a monologue about 'books to publish and deadlines to meet.'

There was more delay while the police prepared her statement. Her hand quivered as she signed it. It was after six when Julie drove her home. Then she had to search for her passport.

'Don't worry love. We'll find whoever did it,' the policewoman said, then left.

That night, hideous images of Henson's mutilated body, bathrooms of blood, Caroline Di Angello and Casper meeting at a lovers tryst, circled round and round in her dreams. At about three thirty, being alone in London, without a shoulder to cry on hit hard. A painkiller induced more fitful dozing, but at dawn she gave up and watched the news on Sky, wrapped in the duvet.

If motivation to get into work was required, the memory of Imogen's tyrannical words provided it. Going sick and being alone in the flat all day had no appeal, so she struggled in, covering up her woes with make-up. All day her nerves were taut like straining wire. Endless black coffee kept her going.

'I warned you there could be trouble in nosing around in all this,' Imogen had begun when she arrived. 'I don't know why you couldn't stick to just doing your job. Trouble is nowadays everybody wants to be so damn clever. In my day you were grateful for a job and did as you were told.'

'If you recall, my original object in this was to try and improve our sales figures,' Jenny retorted. 'You said when I applied for the job that you wanted someone with enterprise and initiative. Well that's what you've got. If it doesn't suit you when I try to apply some of it that's not my fault.' Imogen glared. Jenny responded with her own stony stare.

'When's that proof reading I gave you yesterday going to be finished?' Imogen asked.

'You'll have it by lunchtime,' Jenny replied and stalked out of the room.

Throughout the day a feeling persisted that behind her back everybody was talking about her. Coming in on the tube she had decided not to say anything about Caroline Di Angello and what she'd mentioned about a film for 'Flame in the Sky'. She was in enough hot water already. All she wanted was to let this matter drop and spend the weekend with her family in North Wales.

By five o'clock she was depressed, very tired and ready to slip quietly out of the office. Hurrying along the passageway to the post room, with some letters, she nearly fell into Anthony Rathenberg, who was coming round a corner the other way.

'Miss Millington how clumsy of me,' he said when they had recovered their poise. 'I was so sorry to hear of your predicament with Henson. If you have any problems with the police you must let me know.'

'You're very kind,' she replied, managing a weak smile.

'H'm, you still look a bit shaken. Perhaps one day next week I could treat you to lunch. You can tell me all about it. It might help to get it off your chest.'

'That would be nice.' She felt her face colour red and had to force another smile. The letters gave her the excuse to hurry on.

CHAPTER

DRIVING OUT OF LONDON THE EVENING TRAFFIC WAS HEAVY. JENNY'S small Peugeot dodged from lane to lane to keep ahead of the flow. On the A5 concentration was still required. At Oswestry the countryside took on a more rural aspect and at last she was able to gather her thoughts. By the time she reached the Horse Shoe Pass, just out of Llangollen, London and its hyped up environment seemed complete madness. An image of Henson Littlewood's blood splattered body infiltrated her mind, forcing her to stop in a lay-by and dab at the tears.

She got out for some air. A car hurtled by, the driver tooted his horn and waved; then she realised she was home; nobody waved in London. Not far to go now. Dusk was descending. The road narrowed; hedgerows full of riotous colour were illuminated by her headlights.

Her parents were waiting to greet her at the front door. They'd spotted her lights half a mile away. She was home and fell into their arms. When they all stood in the hall and looked at each other she noticed a little more grey in their features, a few more lines engraved on their faces, but whatever, they were unmistakably her mother and father.

'Plas', a rambling nineteen twenties house, with four draughty bedrooms and commodious living rooms had been home, for all her life. Looking around, nothing much had changed. The same worn carpet covered the stairs and hall. The wallpaper, she remembered her father hanging when she was in school. The banister she and Isabel used to slide down still had a knob missing at the top. Now it all looked tired and dated, but it didn't matter, she felt secure and that evening she was very glad to be there.

'We are relieved to hear you still have your job,' her mother said, when they 'd settled in the lounge. She sat on the settee opposite the two of them. The worn patch where her feet used to rest as a child was still evident. Father was in his favourite armchair, with its pipe stained burns. 'I was beginning to imagine all sorts of things,' mother added.

'There's no need to get worried mother. I have to complete a bit of research up here for an author, that's all.'

'Is it the one you asked me about?' her father cut in.

'Yes Dad, Casper Watkins. Do you remember him now?'

'Sort of. Bright boy, but terribly wicked. As I said on the phone, there was something funny that went on in the family before he was born. They kept it very quiet and despite the rumours nobody got to the bottom of it. Which is unusual for round here.'

Jenny smiled. Her father thrived on gossip. She watched him suck on his pipe, as his mind played with the machinations of what might have occurred.

'The others are coming,' mother said, butting in. 'Duncan had an operation this afternoon, so they won't be here until around midnight. Your father's going to wait up.'

Jenny's heart sank. Any hopes of a relaxing weekend had been dashed. Over dinner, her parents relayed the local gossip. Who'd died, who'd got married and who'd been born. She related snippets of London life; the office, the authors, but omitted to mention anything about Ebury Terrace, or Henson Littlewood.

By the time her sister's family arrived her mother had gone to bed. Jenny and her father had sat up, reminiscing on old times. Just after midnight the doorbell broke the spell and Damien, Scott, Lily, Sebastian, Henrietta and their parents, all burst into the big square hall, like a river in flood, leaving bags, boxes and toys in their wake.

The kids were bright and intelligent, collectively noisy and bristling with their own opinions. Their combined vivacity, however, sometimes grated on Jenny's nerves. Henrietta was the prettiest and Scott the most like his domineering father. Isabel fussed over them all like a bad tempered mother hen, while Duncan ordered them about like a Head Scouter in charge of a boy scout troupe. Visually they were all attractive, which made Jenny wonder why she found it so difficult to get along with them.

'I'll make a pot of tea, then I'm going to bed,' Jenny announced after all the greetings.

Sitting by the Aga, in the kitchen, next morning was like her schooldays. Just her and father, slowly going through the business of breakfast. The others were still in bed. While she tucked into toast he sipped on his coffee, read the newspaper and sucked on his pipe. Eventually the children upstairs, bumping around, reinstated reality.

'I'm going out for a while Dad. See if I can make some headway on this research,' she said. 'Tell Mum I'll be back for lunch.'

He lifted his arm in silent acknowledgement, puffed a cloud of pipe smoke while his eyes remained on the sports page. Jenny smiled and patted his shoulder as she walked past.

Instead of taking the main road, through Mold to Gwernaffield, she took the twisting more picturesque route through the hills and the village of Pantymwyn. When she was a child her father used to own an old Morris with a sunshine roof. Then, the greatest thrill in the world, while he drove through those tortuous lanes, was to stand on the passenger seat, with her head out through the top. The breeze flowing through her hair was a sensation she treasured and never forgot. That morning the sky was bright and clear and the views of Moel Famu and Llys-y-Coed were just as she remembered.

The village square at Gwernaffield contained a pub and two shops; a straight road climbed gently away into the countryside. Driving slowly along it she counted off the houses looking for number thirty one. New bungalows and dormers had been intermingled with the older dwellings since she last came this way. About halfway up, three tiny stone cottages were set back and enclosed by a low dry-stone wall. The properties were unnumbered, but if she'd counted correctly this was Casper Watkin's family home.

She stopped the car and got out. A small, rusty metal gate, that squeaked when she opened, it provided a communal entrance. Each side of the pathway a thicket gooseberry hedge was going wild. It was all a world away from the elegant residence at Ebury Terrace.

An errant climbing rose wandered over the frontage. The middle cottage had a plaque alongside the front door with the name 'Cartref' painted on it in blue letters. She knocked on the door and waited a long time. When the latch was eventually raised her heart was thumping in anticipation. The door opened and to her surprise a short, rotund, middle aged man struggled to scrape it across the flagstone floor.

'I am sorry to trouble you,' Jenny said. 'But is this the home of Mrs Watkins?'

'Mrs Watkins? Yes,' the man replied. He spoke jerkily. There was something funny about his eyes. The right one appeared to look in the opposite direction from the left and he was unsteady on his feet.

'Is she at home?' Jenny asked.

'M-Mummy, in hospital,' the man stuttered. He spoke like a child, stumbling over his words. 'I'm- hu-her- s-son, T-Trevor.' He grinned throughout.

Son, Jenny thought. Her mind tried to claw on the few details she knew. As far as she could recall there had never been any mention of Casper having a brother. The man spoke again. This time his words came in staccato intonation, with long pauses, as though he was struggling to piece them together.

'Mummy- w-went- in ye-yesterday- for tre-treatment,' he said.

Stuck for a response, Jenny's hand searched in her coat pocket for a business card.

'Oh I am sorry to hear that,' she said and held the card out like a peace offering.

'Well my name is Jenny Millington and I work for the publishing house that produces Casper Watkins' books. I'm trying to contact him.'

The man's stubby fingers struggled with the card. He turned it over and over, but made no attempt to read it.

'Casper!!' the man exclaimed, 'is a gu-good-wr'-writer.' The words he spoke were accompanied by snuffling breath. Saliva formed at the corner of his mouth. "We-n-need him-to he-help, please c'-come-in.'

He turned inside and hobbled over the flagstone floor. He was wearing a pair of worn blue slippers with holes at the front through which his toes poked. The door frame was low, the room inside minute. A single window let in what little light there was. Against one wall a Welsh dresser with china and polished brass gave off a bright lustre. A coal fire glowed in a metal grate and a down draught of smoke belched out when Jenny closed the door.

'Is Mrs Watkins all right?' Jenny asked. 'You said she had to go to hospital for some treatment?' They both stood awkwardly, looking at each other. The man had a peculiar manner about him.

'She has to- have ra- ra rad-ium. Every fe-few months. Need- to find- Ca-Casper,' he said.

'Could I possibly sit down?' Jenny asked. 'All this has come as a bit of a shock.' He struggled to move a blanket off one of the chairs, to clear a space for her to sit. He sat opposite her, trying to fold the blanket in half; each attempt ended in failure.

'Trevor, do you mean that Casper doesn't know about his mother's illness?' Jenny said. She spoke the words very slowly while looking into his eyes. They were green, small and sunken into pronounced cheekbones.

' No,' he replied and shook his head vigorously.

'Mother-is in- Den-bigh,' he said, creating two long syllables out of the word. He pointed to a card on the table beside her, causing the blanket to fall off his knees onto the floor.

The card was a notice for Gladys Watkins to attend at Denbigh hospital for treatment; Princess Margaret Ward it said.

Trevor's words and actions didn't synchronise and Jenny was convinced he couldn't read. He wore a grey sweatshirt, brown jogger pants and the worn slippers. Now that she was close she wondered about his age.

Without warning the door opened and a tall, stocky, elderly woman, with tightly permed grey hair blustered in. Another billow of smoke belched from the chimney.

'I thought I heard voices,' she said. 'Trevor, why didn't you tell me you had a visitor?' The accent was North Wales/Liverpudlian. Wearing a blue housecoat, the woman would have been in her early sixties.

'She's from Ca-Ca-Casper,' Trevor replied. Saliva formed again at the corner of his lips.

'Oh I see,' the woman said.

'Not exactly,' Jenny cut in. 'From his publishers to be precise. We are trying to track him down and I was hoping his mother might know of his whereabouts.'

'Well she's not too good at the moment, but we're coping, aren't we Trevor love,' the woman said, looking at Trevor. He grinned and made a gurgling noise.

'So I gather,' Jenny said. 'I wasn't meaning to intrude. Obviously if I'd known she was unwell I wouldn't have called. But Casper has completely vanished and I just thought there may be a chance of finding out a bit more here.'

'I think we would all like to know where he is,' the woman said, looking sternly at Jenny. 'Perhaps I could have a word outside. You didn't mention your name?' Her tone was presumptuous. She walked towards the door and held it open. Smoke billowed again into the room.

'It's Jenny Millington,' Jenny said and produced another business card.

'Well I'm Iris Francis. The lady's leaving now Trevor, say good-bye.'

Trevor grinned, gurgled and said 'Bye' through a mouthful of heavy breathing and saliva. He waved and then bent down for the blanket.

'Miss Millington, I do wish you'd knocked on our door first,' Iris Francis said, when they were outside, and pointed to the adjacent cottage.

'I'm sorry. I had no idea. I wasn't even sure I had the right house. I just knocked on the first door I came to.'

'Well as you see it is very difficult with Trevor. We can't have him being upset, especially with his mother in hospital.' Iris Francis said in a condescending manner.

'Does he have an illness?' Jenny asked.

'He's mentally deficient.'

'If I had known that,' Jenny started to say, before the woman interrupted again.

'Oh fame is an unfortunate appendage,' Iris Francis said. 'We get all sorts calling here, hoping to see that damn man. But it only upsets them in there,' she said pointing at the cottage. 'You'd think with all

33

the money he's made he'd keep in touch with his family.' Scorn filled out every word.

'How does Trevor cope by himself?' Jenny asked.

'My husband and I do what we can.' Her hand pushed at her hair, fluffing it up. 'We've lived next door for twenty years. The lady from the social services comes twice a day, but if they keep Gladys in hospital he'll have to go back to the Home. He can occupy his day, he sketches. He's very talented at that, but he can't look after himself.'

'Oh dear,' Jenny said.

Iris Francis nodded towards Casper's cottage.

'He's lived most of his life in a home, but since Casper stopped coming Gladys has had him here. They're company for each other you see.'

'Jennifer my dear, a detective Ian Roberts has been on the phone from Kensington police station,' her mother said when Jenny walked into the kitchen at 'Plas'. 'He wanted to know if you are staying here for the weekend. Just what is going on?'

Her father was standing by the Aga. Both their faces were covered with worry. Fortunately the others were out, so she sat at the kitchen table and related the details of her involvement with Henson and Casper. She had just finished when they heard her sister's car wheels scrunch on the drive.

'Don't say anything to them,' she said. Her mother's face had turned ashen, her father was chewing fitfully on the end of his pipe.

'Everything will be all right, I promise,' she added, just before the others came in and provided a distraction.

Lunch was taken up with the kids stories of school life. For once, anecdotes of teenage romance took precedence over Duncan and Isabel's social one-upmanship.

'I'm off to my room. Sort out some of my old clothes,' Jenny said as an excuse afterwards. Last night in bed she had started on a Winston Graham novel. Upstairs, in her room, she settled on the quilt, hoping to lose the afternoon in the intricacy of the plot.

It was a lively tale but the events that morning at Gwernaffield soon began to intrude. She felt foolish and silly turning up like that. The bland expression on Iris Francis' face had told her a lot. Imogen Quaith had been quite right. People should stick to doing what they're employed to do. What still upset her most though, was the sight of Henson Littlewood's body, lying in a bath of his own blood. She'd liked Henson. There had been a sort of unspoken compassion about him.

That evening after dinner Jenny persuaded her father to rattle out a few sing-along tunes on the old family piano. They all joined in on 'Delilah' and 'Cwm Rhondda'. A glint in his eyes prevailed as his hands danced over the keys. Jenny thought it inconceivable that one day he wouldn't be around. Before the children went to bed, they all stood in a circle, holding hands and sang 'Yellow Submarine.'

CHAPTER

HE SHIVERED. THE BATHROOM OF THE COTTAGE HAD A COLD DAMP chill about it. A single bar electric fire, high up on the wall, was the only source of heat. When he leant across the mirror to pull on the cord, his reflection made him stare. His hair was unkempt, a stubbled beard did little to enhance his appearance. How Katherine Walker could find anything remotely attractive in what he saw he couldn't imagine. He'd never told her about his fame or occasional wealth and the pseudonym he used for his work. She only knew him as John Watkins, the man who lived in the cottage at the end of the bay.

For a second his memory jolted back two years, to the Literary awards in New York. He had been there to receive his prize for 'Flame in the Sky'. Afterwards he and Caroline watched the telecast on the late night news in their New York hotel. She had swooned at the sight of him in his tuxedo and black tie.

Fortunately, steam from the bath water soon covered the mirror. That afternoon he'd worked hard, planting seed potatoes. While he wallowed in the warm soapy water, he thought about his writing. For some weeks the germ of an idea about a subversive plot to change Britain into a Republic had festered in his head, but whenever he tried to put pen to paper, nothing of any consequence resulted.

After his bath there were still two hours to kill before that nights tryst with Katherine, so he made a pot of tea, found an old exercise book and settled in the worn green settee by the fire, with the intention of getting something down on paper.

The opening lines were a struggle. The first paragraph a nightmare of alterations. Half way through the second, he screwed the page into a ball and threw it on the fire in disgust.

And that's how it had been, ever since that fateful trip to North Wales. Every time he tried to write, it had ended in failure. He sat back in the settee, closed his eyes and tried to recall the events that had brought him to the cottage.

He'd been driving his beloved red Ferrari 456 through the Pass of Glencoe. Out of the corner of his eye he'd caught sight of Caroline Di Angello's shapely legs alongside him. She was stretched out with the seat laid back. At that moment everything in the world had seemed fine. Musing over the things they'd done together in bed the night before, he'd allowed his eyes to remain fixed on her legs a little too long. Suddenly the wheels of the Ferrari were scudding along the roadside scrub.

'What's the matter, where are we?' Caroline cried out.

They'd been to Inverness for a weekend; combining a few days away with a talk to the local literary society. The hospitality had been very good, and what with the malt whisky and then Caroline's bedtime energy, they were late getting up next morning. He was driving too fast, trying to make up time and yanked at the wheel to get the car back on the road.

'It's all right,' he said. 'I just misjudged a bend that's all. We're in Glencoe. If you stay awake for a while you may see what's left of the best bits.'

She yawned and stretched out her arms. 'More grey hills, more damp landscapes,' she said.

He'd so badly wanted to show her his Highlands. In his youth he'd spent months walking those mountains, lodging at Youth Hostels and climbing as many 'Munros' as he could pack into a vacation. The invitation from Inverness had been too good to resist. He still hadn't made a start on a new book and sometimes travel provides inspiration. And Caroline had been so tetchy of late. This film project had become a sore point between them. He really didn't want to get involved and they'd argued a lot. He thought getting away from London and all the pressures would do them both good.

But the beauty of the Highlands had meant nothing to her. All weekend she'd bitched about getting back to the bright lights and her beau monde friends.

'Can't you go a little slower. All this lurching round the bends, means I can't sleep,' she said.

'I am only trying to get you home as quickly as possible.'

'Well I'd like to get there in one piece.'

He eased on the accelerator. Her words about lurching around the bends reminded him of his mother. She used to scold his father about the same thing when they drove through the Horse Shoe Pass at Llangollen. He hadn't been back home in a while and suddenly felt guilty about it.

'Honey, what would you say to spending a night at Llangollen? There's a nice hotel by the river and some super clothes shops. I'll treat you to a new dress. Make up for the weekend.'

'Oh Casper I don't know. I've got a photo session on Wednesday. I'll need to see Justin before then.'

'We'll be back by late Tuesday morning. It's not far from North Wales to London. There's someone I need to see there. It won't take long, I promise.'

Caroline knew nothing about his family, it was of know interest to her, she lived for the moment. If something wasn't in front of her eyes, it didn't stay in her head for long.

'Will it be warmer than Scotland? You didn't tell me I'd need my thermals.'

That was about as much tacit agreement as he was likely to get. She drifted back to sleep and he pressed his foot a little firmer on the accelerator. He loved driving that car at speed. There were some good straight stretches on the way to Stirling and he was really able to give it a whirl.

The Grapes Hotel on the banks of the River Dee was the only four star accommodation in town. In the foyer, Caroline was quick to impress her name on the hard pressed staff and cash in on her celebrity status. She demanded enough large towels to keep the municipal baths going for a week. She required champagne in her room and her clothes pressed before dinner.

'Now honey are you sure you have everything you want?' he said when they were eventually settled in their room. It was the largest they had, with a view of the river.

'Casper these wardrobes don't look clean to me,' she moaned. 'And the bed's so small.' By then the entire contents of her two suitcases were spread over the bed, the chairs and the floor.

'Well you sort it out with reception honey. The bed suits me fine if it means I can be closer to you.'

'How long will you be gone?' she asked.

'Only an hour or so. Why don't you take a look at the shops before you have your bath? See if you can find a little dress. I'll settle the bill when I get back.'

That weekend had brought home a host of realities. In London and the flashy resorts they usually frequented they would mix in cafe society. In those places there was always somebody or something distract her, but alone together like this was a different matter and he was glad of an excuse to slip away.

Exhaust fumes belched, blackening the air, as the Ferrari zoomed out of the hotel car park. The roof opened electronically. He tweaked the accelerator and headed for the countryside he called home.

He couldn't put a date on the last time he'd travelled those roads. Latterly he'd entertained his mother in London, and he reckoned it must have been at least ten years since his last visit.

Swinging around bends at speed, the roads appeared narrower than he remembered, the fields smaller, the cottages minute. His village had changed beyond recognition. Ugly new houses with no style or form predominated. How could they have given planning permission for these, he thought. This was his home, the place he had eulogised about to his chums in London.

Driving up the main road, forlorn, amongst the new clutter, was Mrs Hughes' cottage, once the village farm. Greens fields of pasture and hay had abutted right up to the dry stone wall of his mother's boundary.

Now dormer bungalows in unimaginative rows, with satellite dishes, glared at each other. He used to date Mrs Hughes' daughter, Eira. Together, when they were kids, they climbed Moel Famu.

Outside his mother's cottage there wasn't room to park the Ferrari, so he drove on past, to a spot where there used to be a pull-in to a field. To his dismay the field had become a cul-de-sac. 'Twenty Executive dwellings in a rural aspect' the Agent's elevated board pronounced. A mini roundabout disguised where the pull-in had been.

A tarmacadam pavement, with kerbstones, where wild flowers once flourished in a hedgerow, led him back down the hill past Mrs Thomas' shop. Boarded up, he'd forgotten about the corrugated roof. There, he'd bought his first packet of cigarettes and taken on his first job, delivering newspapers.

The metal gate to his mother's cottage squeaked; a habit it developed after his father's death. He thought the front door needed a coat of paint and wondered if he should knock or breeze in as he'd always done. Hell, he thought, I don't have to knock, this is my home. He lifted the latch and pushed hard, having remembered it dragged on the step.

'Hello mother, are you in?' he called out.

God how small it was. However did we manage. Until he went to University he and his parents had lived comfortably for seventeen years in this tiny room. Five strides took him across the flagstone floor to the kitchen, which remained only a china sink and few old fashioned cupboards. The floorboards creaked above his head.

'Is that you mother? It's the prodigal son, come home,' he called out. The staircase was housed in a gap between the living room and the kitchen. Footsteps padded down the treads.

'How are you my dear?' he asked as the door at the bottom opened. Then to his surprise a strange looking man, with glazed eyes stood facing him.

'Who the hell are you?' Casper asked. The man was wearing a 'Manchester United' sweatshirt and jogger pants.

'Tre-vor,' the man stuttered.

'Where's my mother?'

'Gone- to t-the- s-shops. Be b'back- soon,' the man said. The words eked out slowly.

Casper wondered if he was a burglar, maybe a tramp? His mother had a habit of leaving the front door unlocked. He'd told her about it enough times. But the man seemed unconcerned and shuffled off towards the fire in a pair of broken slippers.

'How long has she been gone?' Casper asked.

'She won't-b'be long.' The man said, he looked agitated and started to shake. Perhaps his mother was looking after him for a friend, Casper thought. He certainly appeared to pose no threat.

'I'm Casper Watkins,' he said. 'I've been up in Scotland and thought I'd pop in and see my mother on the way home.'

The man's eyes lit up. A sort of gurgling sound came out of his mouth and saliva formed at the corner of his lips. 'Ca-Casper. The-writer,' he stuttered.

'Yes, yes, that's me. Are you here for the day? Trevor you said the name was?'

The man gurgled again and nodded his head. 'I- live- with m-mother n-now,' he said and grinned. Then his hands began to fidget nervously.

'You mean you live with your mother?'

Trevor didn't reply.

Casper was confused. He was getting annoyed, but Trevor's body continued to shake, he began to hyper-ventilate. 'Mother-b'back-soon,' he murmured through panting breath.

'All right old chap, calm down. We'll wait until Mrs Watkins gets back,' Casper said.

He sat down in his old chair by the fire while Trevor shuffled in front of him, round and round in circles, in his broken slippers, as though he was doing a slow waltz.

'You- are- very fa-fa-mous?' Trevor said next. He grinned and more saliva formed around his lips.

'Yes, that's right. I live in London now, but this used to be my home,' Casper said spreading his right arm out in an arc.

Trevor continued to move in slow circles. Casper wondered if the man was recovering from a stroke. It didn't make sense though, his mother hadn't mentioned anything about this on the phone when they last talked. Anyway, what was she doing taking in someone at her time of life. She was over eighty years of age.

'Very fa-fa-mous,' Trevor repeated and continued grinning.

'I suppose I am. It's not that important though. Why don't I make us a nice cup of tea,' Casper said, glad of an excuse to go into the kitchen. He was annoyed. His mother wasn't fit enough to go taking people in. Why hadn't she discussed this with him? Surely she was not that short of money to require a lodger?

While the kettle boiled his anger welled. He'd made a special effort to detour this way from Scotland and surprise her. Have a little chat, tell her what he'd been doing. Now there was this fellow hanging around, acting as though he lived here; it just wasn't good enough. He should have kept on for London, could have spared himself another night of Caroline's moaning as well.

The scrape of the front door coincided with the kettle boiling. He reached into the cupboard for another cup.

'There we are now pet, is everything all right?' he heard his mother say. Trevor gurgled something. 'What's the matter?' she added.

When Casper carried the teacups into the room he couldn't believe what he saw. His mother was standing by the fire with her arm around Trevor's shoulders. She looked frail and drawn.

'Mother, it's great to see you. How are you?' he said and put the tray onto the table.

An expression of fear crossed his mother's face. He walked towards her and she fell into his arms.

'How are you then?' he asked. 'I wasn't expecting company. Anyway the wait was worth it. I've brewed some tea.'

'Oh John, you didn't ring,' his mother replied breathlessly. 'You always telephone when you're coming.' Holding her, he could feel how thin she was.

'I came on a whim. I was on my way back from Scotland. Didn't mean to shock you. Thought you'd be pleased to see me. Never mind, let's all have a cup of tea and you can introduce your friend.'

She backed away, her face had coloured crimson. Casper knew she suffered from blood pressure and he was concerned. Suddenly, he felt even more guilty about his protracted absence. Trevor began circling again in front of the fire.

'You'd better sit down dear,' Casper said to his mother. 'You look worn out. I'll get the tea. I do wish you'd get the bus from the village.

I've told you before about that hill with a shopping bag. It's too much at your age.'

Trevor gurgled something. Casper hurried to the kitchen. When he returned with the teapot his mother's face was still very red.

'Now mother, you must introduce me properly to Trevor,' he said, then stirred the tea in the pot.

She sighed heavily before she spoke.

'Oh John, it's such a long story. I don't know where to begin, I do wish you'd phoned.' A weary resignation filled her voice.

Casper poured tea for all of them, added his own milk and sugar, then held out the tray for his mother to do the same. Trevor was still moving in circles. His mother dealt with a cup for him.

'Well I'm here for an hour or so,' Casper began. 'Plenty of time for us all to get acquainted. With my stories I always say you have to start somewhere and the beginning is usually as good a place as any.'

'Come and sit here by me Trevor love and have your tea,' his mother said. She got up, removed her coat and helped Trevor onto the settee alongside her. Then she placed the cup, without the saucer into his hand.

'Now don't spill it,' she said, sat alongside, then sighed again before she spoke.

'Oh John, it's so difficult to explain. It all happened so long ago and you rarely come here these days. There was no need to tell you.'

'Tell me what?' Casper chuckled. 'I'm your son. Surely you can tell me.'

'It's not like that.' His mother paused. 'Trevor, perhaps you'd better take your tea upstairs. Leave John and I to talk for a while. Help him up the stairs with it John, he can't manage.'

Casper took Trevor's cup and held out his free arm, which Trevor used to get on his feet. Then he led, with the cup in hand, up the steep stairs to a tiny bedroom at the back; his bedroom, when he'd lived there. He settled Trevor into a chair. The same chair he used to hang his clothes on. He placed the cup on a small table. The very table he used when he started writing. Scattered across it were the most perfect pencil sketches. He bent over to look. They were all of the view from the window, across the valley to the mountains.

'Is he all right? He looks a bit funny to me,' Casper said when he returned downstairs.

'He's mentally retarded,' his mother said. 'He's been that way all his life.' She was sipping at her tea, her face colour was still high.

'Well what's he doing here? You shouldn't be looking after someone like that at your age.'

His mother finished her tea and set the cup back down on the tray.

'I have to look after him John, he's my son, your half brother.'

'Don't be ridiculous mother. There's only ever been the three of us. You, father and me.' He counted out with his fingers and then held up three. 'You must be getting confused. Somebody hasn't forced you to take him in have they? I'll sort it out if they have.'

'No son, nobody has forced me to take him in.' She shook her head. 'He's here because I asked for him to be here.'

There was another silence. His mother didn't look well, Casper wondered for a second if she was going to pass out.

'Are you sure you're all right mother? Can I get you some more tea?'

'No I don't want anymore tea, son. As I said, it happened so long ago.' She bent her chin into her chest, shaking her head from side to side as she spoke. 'You never come back nowadays and I hoped you'd never find out. There was no need for you to know after all this time. But I was so lonely and it seemed silly to keep him in a Home. I just wanted him with me for these last few years. It's all he's had, you've had all the rest.'

Casper stood in front of her rocking from one foot to the other.

'Tell me mother if I have got this right, or am I going off my head? What you are saying to me is that this chap upstairs,' he said, pointing towards the bedroom, 'is in some way related to me?'

'He's my son!' his mother said. Her voice was choking with emotion. 'He was born before you.' Tears began to tumble down her lined face.

'Why was I never told about this? What's so terrible that you and father couldn't tell me about a handicapped child? It's not that uncommon.'

His mother buried her head in her hands and began sobbing.

'Mother, I must know,' Casper bellowed.

'He's not your father's son.' The words came out like an anguished cry.

'What?'

The door at the bottom of the stairs squeaked and when Casper looked round Trevor was standing in the room, gurgling and hyperventilating.

'It's all right Trevor love,' his mother said through her sobs. 'There's no need to fret.' She struggled to her feet and went over to him, looped her arm inside his and guided him back to the settee.

'As I said John,' she began, when Trevor had sat down. 'It all happened a long time ago, at the start of the war. Your father was away at sea and I met a man. We fell in love. These things happened.' She sat down alongside Trevor. 'They were such crazy times son. None of us knew what we were doing. The war made life a mess.' She was shaking her head again. 'Trevor is that man's son. His father was killed by a land mine, in France, before he was born.'

Casper made no comment. His head moved from one side to the other, staring at them both in turn.

'He's always been like this,' his mother said and looked at Trevor, then rubbed his arm. 'They put him in a Home when he was six months old, because his father was killed on active service. It was the war son.'

'I don't believe what I'm hearing here Mother? Do you mean to tell me you had an illegitimate son and in all this time nobody has known. Not even my father?'

'Your father was away for five years John. He was missing for two. I never believed he'd come back. The army looked after Trevor. There was no need to tell your father. And then we had you. Times were bad. We were all just grateful to get out of it alive.'

Casper could feel his chest tightening. The room was stifling, he felt sick. He had to get outside before he did something stupid. He bolted for the door. On the way, his arm caught the tray and one of the cups crashed to the flagstone floor, shattering into pieces.

Outside he stood by the dry stone wall, looking across the valley. Sweat poured off his forehead. He wanted to be sick, but couldn't organise the bodily function. Instead he just stood, sweating and shaking, like a dog coming out of a river.

He was like that for a long time, lost in a state of inertia. Then moisture dripping from his hair into his eyes brought him round. At first he thought it was sweat, but it was rain, he needed shelter. He couldn't go back inside. Round the back of the cottage was a garden shed. He headed that way, stumbling past the outside privy, down a steep slope to a picket gate and a vegetable plot, once his father's pride and joy. Overgrown with weeds, it looked desolate.

A wooden peg in a metal eye held the door to the shed closed. Warped by damp, it creaked when he pulled it open. Inside, garden tools lay on the bench, as though his father had gone for lunch and would be back afterwards. A pair of shears were clamped in a vice, ready for sharpening. A seed tray half filled with compost, anticipating the rest. In the middle of the bench, covered in mould and dust, was his fathers flat hat. He picked it up and ran his fingers round its rim.

Holding it close, he tried to comprehend what he had just been told, while rain tip-tapped on the felt roof. Slowly he allowed his brain to filter out the emotion. Then, he realised, what all these years, he had once considered right, suddenly appeared wrong and what he had thought of as wrong, was now not quite as wrong as it might have seemed before.

Through the shed window he could see the lump of hill, half way across the valley, they used to call the 'tumpeth'. As a young lad he would sit at his bedroom window and watch the spring lambs frolic there in the early evening sunlight. His father used to come home from work that way. When he appeared on the 'tumpeth' Casper would call out and wave. His father would wave back and then Casper would run down the narrow staircase to greet him at the back door.

Carefully, he replaced the hat where it had been on the bench, and walked out of the shed. Re-inserting the wooden peg was like closing a lid on a box of secrets. Going in there had been a flight home, to a world of magic, a world of dreams and simple pleasures, a world he had forgotten, a world that no longer existed, but a world that at one time had meant everything.

In the cottage his mother was sweeping the broken cup from the floor. Trevor was still sitting on the settee.

'Let me do that mother. That won't help your blood pressure,' Casper said.

'It's all right son. We have to manage.'

Pain clouded their eyes while they stood looking at each other. Words were superfluous but were necessary to go on.

'I just called here to check you were all right,' he said. 'Now I see you are,' he nodded at Trevor. 'I'm happy.'

'Don't think badly of me John. What's done is done. It never affected your life. You've been such a success. What was the point in telling you?'

'Perhaps you might have given me the opportunity to decide if it mattered mother, that's all.'

Her face was colouring up again. 'I just did what I thought was best for everybody. I am sorry to cause you so much upset.' The tears began to well again, Trevor was fidgeting, becoming edgy.

'I know mother, I know.' They hugged and her damp face buried into his chest. 'I must be getting back,' he said. 'There's someone waiting for me at the hotel.'

'Now that you and your father are gone, Trevor is all I have. You must see that John. We have to do the best we can for each other. Live our lives for each day. Try and remember that son.'

'Yes mother.'

That tiny cottage, in the North Wales hills, had been his home for twenty years. It had provided his roots, established his foundation, but at that moment it felt alien and he couldn't stay another minute.

'I'll give you a call when I'm back in London mother, I promise. All this'll have had time to sink in by then.' They were still holding each other. Her eyes pleaded for contrition, but the right words wouldn't come and he headed for the door. 'I promise I'll phone,' was all he could manage. He raised his right hand in a half wave as he pulled the door closed.

'God bless son,' he heard his mother call out.

Driving back to Llangollen, an image of Trevor holding onto his mother's arm, blurred his vision. He was addled, drove too fast, there were a couple of near misses on the bends with other cars, and the last person he needed to face in that frame of mind was Caroline Di Angello.

Wrapped in a white bath robe she lay on the quilt of the bed, like a temptress waiting for her prey, when he walked into their room. He noticed a bucket of champagne on the bedside table.

'There you are sugar,' she said. 'You have been gone a long time? I was beginning to wonder if you had another woman. An old flame, perhaps?' Her eyes fluttered, a provocative grin spread across her face.

The sickly squirm of her words grated in his brain. On any other day they would have drifted over his head. He would have mouthed back some meaningless platitudes, indulged her fantasies and treated her like the spoilt, pampered, over-sexed starlet she was.

'I thought you were going shopping?' he said, moving across the room. 'Haven't you got anything better to do than laze around all afternoon?'

Cold daggers of steel shot from her eyes.

'If you must know, I have been out. I've been looking around this god forsaken town all afternoon. But there's nothing here I'd want to touch with a barge pole. I wouldn't be seen dead in the clothes on offer here. They're like you, boring and dull.'

'Oh go to hell you stupid bitch,' he said and stomped towards the door. He was just in time. Caroline hurled a champagne glass at him. It missed his head by inches and smashed against the door as he pulled it closed.

A winding pathway through the hotel gardens led down to the river. He followed its loosely chipped trail, past the rhododendrons and azaleas; moisture from the days rain dripped off their leaves. His body was shaking with anger and he took deep breaths. 'You can't go on like this John,' he remembered saying to himself. Below his feet swirled the River Dee. The last few hours had stripped away the structures of his life. Now that he was down to the bare bones, he considered there was very little worth preserving. He spent a long time on the banks of the Dee contemplating his fate.

It was past six when he looked at his watch. He ran back up the path. The hotel bar had a dark blue carpet and oak panelled walls, wood smoke drifted from a canopy fireplace. He stopped in his tracks when he saw the back of the familiar blonde head. She was sitting on a bar stool, wearing a mini skirt that struggled to cover her backside. Her steady gaze was fixed on a dark haired young barman, who was nervously polishing a wine glass.

'There you are Caroline,' Casper said. 'I've been looking everywhere for you.'

'Yes, here I am, but you needn't have worried, Gareth here has been looking after me very well. He does the most marvellous things with Gin and Tequila. He's promised to show me more later on.' Her words were slurred.

Gareth looked away embarrassed, and kept on polishing.

'You had better make it a large one of whatever it is, then please Gareth,' Casper said. 'Seems like I've got a lot of catching up to do. Another for you my dear?'

He remembered very little about the rest of that evening and the night that followed. At some time or another he could recall being in the pseudo glazed opulence of the hotel dining room, but how or what they ate he didn't know. He did remember waking up next morning with a blinding headache and Caroline's blonde tresses on the pillow alongside.

CHAPTER

CAROLINE AND CASPER EXCHANGED FEW WORDS ON THE JOURNEY BACK from Llangollen. Only the thumping beat of the music she chose on the car stereo broke the silence. He deposited her outside her Bloomsbury apartment block and drove away without entering into any further arrangements.

At home, in Ebury Terrace, he put on some Vivaldi, rewound his answer phone, and delved into his mail. Amongst the phone messages was one from Henson and another from a man with an American accent he didn't recognise. He rewound the spool and listened more carefully. A name he couldn't recall asked him to urgently ring a mobile number. To hell with it he thought; probably a magazine trying to arrange an interview. He poured a whisky then settled at his desk.

The weekend and all its events had left his brain whirling like a merry-go-round. There and then he decided to offload Caroline's cargo of wantonness; she'd become too much of an intrusion. His mother and this business in North Wales was a different matter. There was nothing he could do there; what was done was done.

He needed to settle back into his writing. For that a clear mind was essential. How to attain it was the problem. Perhaps his friend Ivan could help? Ivan had always lived on the edge. A playwright and a poet, he'd never really been part of anything, yet he always seemed to be at the centre of everything. They'd met at a literary party in Chelsea.

'How've you been this long time man?' Ivan replied when Casper phoned. His dialect was South Wales, mid west South Wales, Neath to be precise. But he laced it with an Afro-Caribbean vocabulary. Ivan had lived in communes, championed every conceivable underground cause and they'd all added discernible influences to his style.

'Been trying to keep out of trouble Van,' Casper replied. 'Unfortunately nowadays that's not easy.'

'You're right there man, you're dead right there. Anyway what can I do for you Casper?'

'Need your help Van. Question of the mind. Needs clearing out, to create some space for the writing.' They talked some more and arranged to meet for lunch next day.

Casper pulled the phone from the socket. He would return Henson's call in the morning. Topping up his whisky he carried the glass and the bottle into the bathroom.

All day he'd savoured the thought of lying suspended in the surreal motion of his new whirlpool bath, a recent addition in the guest bathroom. He hummed to himself while slurping whisky as the water filled. Then, once he was fully immersed, the warm churning water, together with the mellowing affect of the whisky, encouraged sleep. Later, in the sanctuary of his huge circular bed, it came like a drug, anaesthetising the jagged edges of his mind.

A continuous ringing in his head brought him around. He rubbed his scalp and bumped his head up and down on the pillow, trying to alleviate the sensation. Three or four times he tried, but the ringing continued. Consciousness brought a searing headache which sliced across his forehead.

'Where am I?' he thought. 'Hell, that must be my bloody doorbell.' Through bleary eyes he looked at his bedside clock. Nine thirty was showing; daylight poured in through the bedroom window, it was morning.

The door bell kept ringing.

'All right, all right, I'm coming,' he yelled, while searching for his dressing gown. The bell was still grating in his head. 'Stop that bloody ringing,' he shouted as he headed for the hall. In the mirror he looked lousy. The previous day he'd had no real food; the headache was making him nauseous.

When he opened the door Caroline was standing outside with two tall, dark haired, snappily suited young men, carrying briefcases.

'Casper, where the hell have you been?' she said, glaring at him. 'I tried telephoning you all last night. And I've been ringing this damn bell for the last ten minutes.'

'Persistent aren't you,' he said and looked in turn at the three of them.

She had tinted her hair and fluffed it up. Justin of course, Casper thought. A white halter top displayed her cleavage; shiny, tight fitting, black slacks emphasised the rest.

'Casper what have you been doing with yourself, you look awful,' she said, then swept past him into the hall. Her perfume compounded the nausea in his stomach; the two sidekicks followed on behind and they all trooped through into the lounge.

'Do come in,' Casper said, still holding onto the door. He closed it and shook his head.

'I'm sorry we haven't been introduced,' he said when he caught up. The men were in their early thirties, both over six foot tall. They wore dark suits and white shirts, with button down collars; they looked bright and shiny like newly minted coins.

Caroline looked Casper up and down like a piece of dirt, before her hand motioned in the direction of the young men.

'Casper, this is Daryll and Brad. They've flown all the way from Los Angeles to see you. That's why I've been phoning.' She flashed her alluring page three smile at him.

The two men grinned simultaneously; a toothpaste advertising executive sort of grin. They both said 'Hi' in unison. It looked as though they were about to offer him the opportunity of a lifetime, so he cut in.

'Well it's nice to meet you guys, but as you see I am not really dressed for company. Whatever it is you're selling, I assure you this is not the best time of day to catch me in.'

'No, no, Casper, you don't understand,' Caroline said. 'These are the two men who represent the consortium we met in New York. You know, the one's who want to make a film of your book.'

His headache was hurting like hell. Standing there in his dressing gown and slippers he felt ridiculous.

'Well just to correct Caroline,' the one called Brad drawled, the accent was somewhere between Texas and the West Coast, 'we're actually the account executives attached to this project. We represent S and B Germain Incorporated. It was Mister Schultz and Mister Brannigan who you met in New York. They're our principals. It's our job to evaluate the project.'

'There we are Caspy, I told you so,' Caroline said. In all the time they'd known each other, she'd never ever called him Caspy. Silly cow, he thought. Anger now added to the acidity in his stomach.

'What you mean is, you guys want my money as well as my story?'

'We just want to maximise your opportunities Casper,' the one who was called Daryll said. He had a slight lisp.

Casper had heard enough. When anybody used that sort of gobbledegook it closed his mind.

Then the doorbell rang again. Casper gestured and Caroline bustled away to answer it. Her slacks made a swishing noise as she moved. The three men stood looking at each other in embarrassed silence, until Henson breezed in. He was wearing a khaki safari jacket, with pockets at the front, like a door shoe holder.

'My God, look what the cat's brought in,' Casper said. 'Why don't we make it party?'

'Looks like you're all ready dressed for it sweetie,' Henson replied.

'What the hell brings you here?' Casper said.

'As your Agent I thought I should be here to represent you. You know you haven't a head for figures.'

'Vultures and parasites. I'm surrounded by vultures and parasites,' Casper said.

'Casper why don't you go and change,' Caroline said. 'I'll make some coffee.'

'Why does everybody try to tell me what to do all the time,' he muttered and headed for the bedroom.

When he returned they were all sitting drinking coffee and supping at his brandy. The two Americans looked neat together in the chaise longue. Casper had an idea Henson was eyeing them up.

Caroline sidled up with his coffee.

'There we are. That's much better. You look nice now,' she said and stroked his hair. This is all a game to her, he thought. He realised then that the contrived passion of the last few weeks had been just a ruse to get him to part with his money, for this 'Pie in the Sky' project, as he'd once called it.

'I really feel you guys are wasting your time on this,' he said. 'In some drunken moment, in New York, I may have expressed an interest but in the cold light of day I don't know if want my work debased in celluloid.'

'Ah, the author's pride,' Henson cut in. 'Just think of the wider audience dear boy.'

'When I want your advice I'll ask for it,' Casper said. 'Just remember, without me you starve.'

'That's exactly what I was thinking dear boy. We haven't had a new book in three years.'

'Come on Caspy, we could all have such a great time doing this together,' Caroline said. She'd poured him a brandy, placed it alongside him on his desk, then rubbed the back of his head.

Brad's hands had a habit of gesticulating before he talked. Up until then he'd said very little, but suddenly his hands began to oscillate, as though he was beginning a mime.

'Now Casper I know how you must feel about this,' he began. 'We accept that 'Flame in the Sky' is your baby.' The hands were still working. 'We are not trying to impose ourselves on your work. It's a great story. S and B Germain will produce a product we can all be proud of. But, by putting up some capital you can retain control on the artistic side. It's a gigantic opportunity to present your work to a mass audience. Critical mass is what counts nowadays.'

Henson and Caroline were nodding their heads. Casper slurped at the brandy, then began to paraphrase Brad's transatlantic jargon.

'I might take a rain check on the idea Brad. Just not switched into that mode at the moment. I think there is another window I may pursue,' he said mockingly.

Henson sniggered.

Daryll reached into his briefcase and pulled out a sheaf of papers. Caroline crossed and uncrossed her legs, shook her hair and then began fingering at the tresses.

Daryll spoke again.

'Look Casper, I've prepared some figures. We could clear thirty million on this. At least look at the projections. If this is a success all your work could be presented through this medium. Think of the fame. Think of the money. You could have homes like this all over the world,' he said sweeping his arm in the air.

'I don't know whether I want homes all over the world. I'm happy as I am. What's money anyway?'

Daryll passed him the wad of papers, bound in an orange folder. Casper flicked over the pages and looked at the Americans. The wide grins were now permanently fixed.

'You'll miss a golden opportunity Casper.' Daryll said. The lisp seemed to accentuate his name. 'I guess we've called at an inopportune time. We'll leave the papers with you. If you're interested give us a call. We're staying at the Hilton.'

'I'll see,' Casper replied. 'But I'm really not bothered.'

Brad stood up and leaned over Casper.

'Here's my card,' he said. Casper caught a whiff of his aftershave. 'Give us a call anyway.' The drawl sounded good on the word 'call.'

Henson escorted the Americans to the door. The sublime expression on Caroline's face changed as soon as they disappeared into the hall.

'You are a damn fool,' she began. 'This is the most tremendous opportunity for all of us. Can't you see that.'

'Can't see how it concerns you my dear. It's my story they want and my money. Don't see how it suddenly becomes all of us, as you put it.'

'I'm obviously wasting my breath. This was something we could have all done together.'

'Perhaps that's what puts me off the idea.'

She stared at him. A stare of venom and loathing. He could almost detect her blood boiling in front of him. Henson came back into the room.

'Caroline's just leaving,' Casper said. 'While you're on your feet old chap, perhaps you could see her out as well.'

She continued to glare.

'Oh I'm going all right. You've been fortunate up to now. Just don't come running to me when you're down on your luck. Next time you're looking for a quick fix, don't look in my direction.'

'I shan't.'

She was standing over him. Her sexuality, her desire, her passion, every pore in her body bristled with intimidation. He wanted her now. She must have read his mind.

'Anyway, you're a lousy lover,' she said. 'Justin makes up for your deficiencies. Don't worry Henson, I can find my own way out. I always said he was only a glorified scribbler.'

She stalked out and slammed the door. The vibration activated the bell. The two of them looked at each other.

'Women eh,' Casper said. 'You're better off without them my friend.'

'Maybe dear boy, maybe,' Henson replied. He poured himself another brandy and sat at the chaise longue where the Americans had been.

'It's an idea you ought to think about though old chap. You've nothing in the pipeline. It would fill in a couple of years while you put together another book.'

'I couldn't stand all that nonsense. You heard the things they said. Could you imagine me getting involved with that lot. Drive me round the bend in a week.'

'Well you wouldn't have to do a lot. Films are different. Just be a consultant. Look over the script and that sort of thing. Be a marvellous investment for your money as well. You're not making much on it at the moment. The story's good enough to stand by itself.'

'I don't know old friend. Just not my scene really. Better off sticking to what we know, eh.'

'Well you know best, you always have. But you really ought to start a new book.'

'I know, I know. Need to get my mind clear, that's all, old pal. This brandy's good isn't it.'

CHAPTER

CASPER WAS LOOKING FORWARD TO HIS LUNCH WITH IVAN. SOON AFTER Henson left he began to search his wardrobe for something appropriate to wear. An old kaftan he'd bought in the market at Portobello Road seemed suitable. Caroline said it made him look like a nineteen sixties hippy. That and a wide brimmed leather hat, acquired when they'd been racing together at Kempton Park, would at least ensure he didn't look like a member of the establishment, something Ivan despised.

Ivan's home was only a few stops away on the tube. Steep concrete steps took him down to the basement apartment of a large terraced house. The door knocker was carved like a serpent's head. Casper could hear the thumping beat of Bob Marley's rhythm as he waited outside.

Ivan Gareth Jones was from Briton Ferry; a working class area of steel people, located between Neath and Port Talbot. In those towns they built a special breed of man. As a schoolboy he'd been a tearaway. Fights, gangs, trouble with the law, all occupied his adolescence. He joined the parachute regiment and to some extent everything changed. He served in Northern Ireland and was seconded to the SAS, working undercover, trying to infiltrate an IRA cell. But in the end he bought himself out; the contradiction in principles were just too much for him to condone.

'Got some new sounds on the speakers I hear?' Casper said, when Ivan opened the door.

'Good social commentator Mr Marley. How have you been this long time Casper?'

'Struggling Van, struggling.'

Ivan's middle aged appearance always took Casper by surprise. Fuzzy, greying, fair hair, was tied back into a pony-tail with an elastic band. Metal framed glasses, just as John Lennon wore, were perched precariously on the end of his hooked nose. A black body warmer, over a 'Save the Whales' tee shirt and jeans clothed his tall, thickset body. Summer and winter he always wore army boots. 'Given them when I left,' he'd said. 'The only bloody thing I ever got from the army for nothing.'

The apartment was basically one large room. A bicycle lent against the far wall. An electric sun bed occupied a corner. Ivan's army sleeping bag lay on top of a camp bed; posters espousing Greenpeace, Whales, Kosovo and Chile bombarded your eyes from all the walls.

A massive desk, with cupboards and drawers, front, back and around all the sides dominated the middle of the room. Newspapers, scripts of his plays, copies of his poems, manuscripts from unknown authors looking for his sponsorship, littered the desktop. A bank of computer terminal screens were alight on a table against the far wall. Ivan was an internet freak; at night he surfed the world. He once told Casper he'd broken into the system of MI5 when they were tracking him. 'As a radical activist, I've attracted their attention,' he'd said.

Ivan sat down on a wooden revolving chair on one side of the desk and beckoned Casper to a chair on the other. 'What gives man?' he inquired.

'Not quite sure Van. Going through a stage where I can't seem to write.'

'Well there you have it man,' Ivan said. 'One minute I see you on the television receiving an award for your writing, next minute you're on some quiz show, acting like a music hall entertainer.'

'Necessities of earning a living.'

'Pah!' Ivan replied.

A guest in Ivan's flat was offered brandy, with fresh cherries, in the same way anybody else would offer coffee. He poured two shots from a decanter into wine glasses, adding a cherry to each.

'Your mind can only become institutionalised mixing with that lot,' Ivan continued and spat a pip from one of the cherries into his hand. 'I'll lend you one of Tom Lehr's tapes. Old Tom will put you right. He knew.'

Casper took a sip of his drink. The cherries were slightly chilled.

Behind the desk was a set of library shelves Ivan had rescued from a demolition site. Books, tapes, and pictures bulged haphazardly from it at all angles. Ivan reached backwards amongst them. 'You can borrow that,' he said throwing a tape on the desk. 'Seems to me that your mind's cluttered with frivolities. No space for anything creative.'

They talked some more around the subject and drank more brandy. When hunger intruded, they walked two blocks to an Indian restaurant and continued their dialogue, while curry and red wine blew away the inhibitions.

'London's like a village,' Ivan said. 'Everybody knows how to get at you. In the end, everything becomes too familiar, too comfortable, too habitual.'

'Maybe you're right,' Casper replied.

'Get yourself on the road man. Find a new by-way. Allow some fresh thoughts to come in.'

Casper liked that idea. A complete break. Perhaps a change of scene, change of people, maybe no people at all. That sounded even better. No trappings as well. But where?

For an hour or more the two of them roamed over the subject, while the red wine doused the gastronomical fire of the curry sauce. Ivan talked about his home and the land to its west. A land of history, a land of Merlin, priests and rocky inlets. A countryside abound with folklore, spirits and wild seas. A people who had more in common with Ireland than England. Casper's imagination was stirred.

On the streets around Ivan's flat, on the way back, the man was like a politician on a walkabout. He talked to everybody. No matter what colour or creed; he charmed, he discussed, he dissected their problems with concerned interest. For over an hour he argued, sympathised, cajoled, pleaded, harangued. By the time they reached the apartment, Casper was exhausted.

'Feel I'd better go while I can still stand,' was Casper's reply, when invited in. They made big plans to meet again and continue with the therapy.

Two calls on his answer phone when he got back helped Casper with his decision. One was from Daryll, hoping he'd had time to look at the figures. 'It's a challenge we feel you should take on,' he said. 'We'll call on you on our way to the airport, tomorrow afternoon. Try and give it some quality thought,' he added, before he rang off.

The other was from Henson. 'Give us a call when you get in old pal. Been thinking a bit more about this film business. There's some other people, a European consortium, who may be interested, if you're not fussy about the Americans. They might do a better job anyway. It's only a thought. How was Ivan the terrible?'

Casper really didn't want to get involved in a film of any sort. He wanted to write. Something new, something original. Something about spirits and ghosts and generations of families with evil doings. Something affected by nature, time and tides, mists and religious sects. Something he needed to explore by himself. So he pulled the phone cord out of the socket.

In his bookshelves was an atlas. He found the pages relating to Wales and searched for the places Ivan had mentioned. The map showed there were good roads from London. No, he couldn't take his Ferrari down there. Too obvious, too identifiable. Somebody would spot him. He didn't want that. Peace, isolation and seclusion was what was needed. Make a brand new start.

What about the train? he thought. Yes, that's it, he'd go by rail. The map indicated a line that seemed to run nearly all the way there. He'd travel light, with just a holdall, just like Sal Paradise in Jack Kerouac's 'On the road'. Discover a new world; get everything he needed there; see what life brings. Money's no problem.

He left next morning, before dawn.

CHAPTER

AFTER HER WEEKEND AWAY WORK ON MONDAY MORNING WAS BEGINNING to grate on Jenny's nerves. The office was busy, the telephone didn't stop ringing. She decided to say nothing about her discovery in North Wales and let her idea about finding Casper slide into insignificance.

'Yes, fiction,' was her rather flippant response when the phone jangled yet again. Buried beneath a pile of manuscripts on her desk, she had to fumble around to find it.

'Is that Miss Millington?' a voice said. She was holding the hand-piece between her shoulder and ear, while still writing with her other hand, which made it difficult to hear.

'That's correct,' she responded in an offhand manner.

'It's Anthony Rathenberg, Miss Millington. I was wondering if I could treat you to lunch.'

The muscles in her shoulder contracted in surprise, the phone hand-piece clattered onto the desk.

'I do apologise Mister Rathenberg,' she stuttered retrieving it. 'That's very kind of you. I'd love to have lunch.'

'Fine. There's a little Italian restaurant on the Hanwell Road. It's called the 'Palermo'. It's only a block away. I'll meet you outside at one o'clock, if that's all right.' She agreed and he rang off.

With everything that had happened, she'd completely forgotten about Anthony Rathenberg's proposition for lunch. At the time she'd dismissed it as a bit of office politics, to avoid talking about the weather. Now she was lumbered and totally unprepared.

At a quarter to one she was in the ladies room, repairing her make-up and attacking her hair. Whichever way she combed, it didn't seem to improve things much. She wasn't really dressed for lunch, not with the managing director anyway. Too late to do anything about it now, she thought. He was waiting on the pavement outside when she reached the 'Palermo'.

'Ah there you are Jenny,' he said when she approached. His fair hair fluttered in the breeze. 'What a smart suit,' he continued. 'By the way, please call me Tony. Out of the office we're a first name family.'

She felt flustered. A gust of wind blew her hair all over the place. Inside the restaurant Rathenberg's aplomb was effortless. He was obviously known; the waiters used his name. They were guided to his 'favourite table'. She wondered if he made a habit of taking the young girls from the office out to lunch.

'I must say you do look stunning,' he said when they sat down. 'If I'd known we had such a dazzler in our fiction department I'd have been a more regular visitor to the second floor.'

She blushed heavily and tried to hold onto her composure. 'The tagliatelle is very good and the veal,' he advised as they were inspecting the menu, but she made her own choice. By the time the drinks arrived she felt a little more in control.

'Tell me Jenny, do we have any good new works coming through?' he asked as he sipped at his gin. 'I'm sure Imogen's told you, our figures are slipping. We really do need a couple of new blockbusters.' His deep blue eyes honed in on her. She watched his hands play with his drink glass. He had long, masculine fingers and just for a second she imagined them sensuously roaming her body, then instantly dismissed the image as being preposterous.

'I've read a lot of good things recently,' she replied hesitatingly. 'Unfortunately, they're not what the public seems to want. The type of book that sells is not necessarily the best work we see.'

'H'm, I keep telling my father that. Trouble is, nowadays he gets so irritable. He expects things to be as they were. He won't accept the changes there's been. I suppose I'll be the same one day.'

They talked some more, around the same subject, until their food arrived. She had the pollo al la crema and his was a veal dish swimming in a sauce. He was very easy to talk to, although she realised he was testing her all the time. He made it all seem like relaxed conversation, but he was testing just the same. His eyes constantly possessed an interested attention when she talked and she became entranced by their sparkle.

'On Friday you mentioned you were heading North for the weekend? Did you manage to make it?' he said.

'Just about. Although the way the police behaved over Henson, I had my doubts right up until the last minute.'

'Yes, yes. That must have been horrible for you. If they become aggressive you must let me know. We have a company lawyer. If they want to see you again, I can arrange for the lawyer to be with you.'

'You are kind but I hope they'll leave me alone now. I was beginning to think they thought I did it. If they persist I might shout for help.'

'Please do, it's not a problem. Did you manage to get anywhere with your inquiries on Casper?'

Feeling a little more relaxed she was able to look at him closely. She had never met a man before with such a marvellous cut to his jaw line. It was smooth and even, like the edge of a table. And his eyes had crows feet at their edges, they wrinkled when he smiled. She pretended to chew hard on a piece of chicken before answering his question.

'Well I found his home,' she said eventually. 'But it was all locked up. I knocked on next door and they hadn't seen him for years. They said his mother was in hospital.' She kept her eyes fixed on her plate while she spoke.

'Oh dear, I'm sorry to hear that. If only that man would surface. He could be our saviour. He writes a marvellous tale, just the right style for today's market. All this business with poor Henson does make you wonder though,' he said shaking his head.

'H'm,' Jenny said. 'They were great friends. When I saw Henson, he believed Casper was still around. Just gone to ground somewhere, he said.'

'There we are then. Let's hope this unfortunate business brings him out of his lair. I've arranged for some background details of their relationship to be released to the press. You know, old university chums, long-standing Agent, that sort of thing. Might do the trick; bring Casper to the surface.' The sparkle was back in his eyes. 'You were very brave to get involved.'

'Let's just say I enjoy a challenge,' she said.

He was staring at her and she could feel herself blush again.

'Tell you what,' he said. 'Why don't you come down to my house for the weekend. We're having a little soiree. Just the family and some literary people. Give you a chance to unwind.' His eyes hardened in again.

'Oh you are so kind.' Suddenly she was embarrassed and had to think quickly. 'It sounds marvellous. I'd love to come, but I've promised my sister I'd baby-sit for her this weekend. Her husband's a surgeon and they're off to a medical conference.'

'Oh what a shame. Can't you get out of it. It would be nice for me to have some glamour around.'

'Oh Tony, I'm sure you have all the glamour you want.'

He laughed. The dimples in his chin puckered. She fancied him like mad, but he was really way out of her league.

One evening, later in the week, she was sitting in her flat listening to Catatonia on her CD when the phone rang. It was after ten o'clock. She half expected it to be her mother, still fretting about her involvement with the police.

'Jenny, it's Tony Rathenberg. I'm sorry to ring so late but I've been in a meeting all day.'

'Oh hello,' she replied, too shocked to say more.

'I was wondering if I could change your mind about the weekend. The weather forecast looks good. You told me at lunch you used to ride. Well my father's got a couple of new geldings that need running out. Be great if you could give us a hand.'

'Tony how did you get my number?'

'I looked it up in the telephone directory. Jenny it's lovely over the Sussex Downs this time of year. Do you good after all the trauma with Henson.'

She hesitated. Part of her wanted to go, just for the devilment of it; have some fun for a change and he was right, it would do her good after what she'd been through.

'Tony it's very kind of you, but I can't go back on my word. I told you, I've already promised my sister.'

She didn't know why she was persisting with this lie. The man was certainly attractive and he obviously fancied her, and a weekend at the family home could only enhance her career.

'Oh, I did enjoy our lunch so much,' he said. He sounded disconsolate. She guessed he wasn't used to being turned down.

'Tony you know I'd love to come, but I can't let her down at this late date.'

'Perhaps I could arrange for a baby sitter, to fill in. Where does she live?'

'Glasgow!' she said.

'Oh well, I tried. Perhaps another time?'

'I would really love that Tony. Thank you,' she said and he rang off.

His call at that late hour unsettled her. She paced up and down, with their conversation was still swirling in her head. She thought about his blue eyes, the soft melting tones of his assured words, the cut of his jaw and it all got out of control. She reached into the fridge, poured a large Martini, then continued pacing.

If he'd found her number in the directory, he'd know her address as well and he seemed a persistent type. What would happen if he turned up here at the weekend and uncovered her lie? Her career would be in tatters.

Next morning, by the time the dawn light drifted in through her thin net curtains, she'd formulated a plan. Her trip home the previous weekend had opened her eyes to the unspoilt countryside of her homeland. There was so much she'd never seen. She didn't want to travel North again. Too many temptations there to have another look at Casper's home and stick her nose in where it wasn't wanted. It was an issue she must let go of. There'd been enough grief already.

So she decided to go west for the weekend. The M4 from London and the new Severn Bridge made the shoreline of West Wales accessible. She'd heard so much about it. This was a good opportunity to take a look.

CHAPTER

THE MOTORWAY THROUGH WALES WAS GOOD. SPEEDING PAST THEIR numbered junctions, she ticked off the towns and cities of Newport, Cardiff, Bridgend and Swansea along its route. The road seemed to reach out, like the tentacles of an octopus, and drag Jenny deeper into the bosom of her homeland. Originally, she was planning to venture no further than Swansea, but the setting red sun was a magnet, pulling her further west. The road was clear, the Peugeot revelled in the flow, so she kept her foot hard down on the accelerator.

By ten o'clock she was very tired and began to worry about somewhere to stay. The motorway had ended an hour ago; now there were narrow lanes similar to those in North Wales. The last time she consulted the map, the coast was about twenty miles away, but in the dark it was difficult to judge distances.

Suddenly the road plummeted down a steep hill and came to a dead end, with a collection of cottages round a grassy square. Looking through the car window, in the gloom, she could see an un-modernised pub, an antiquated shop/ post office and a low sea wall.

She ventured warily into the pub. Inside, a Friday night darts match filled the bar. Sandwiches and beer cluttered the tables; men, exuding testosterone, were noisily gathered around the oche. Most of them leered at her when she walked in. She had to shout to make the landlord understand, but yes, they did have a room. Self consciously, she traipsed back to the car for her bag. With every step she could feel the men's eyes on her back. When everything was in, she purchased a drink. 'We'll see you to your room love, if you like,' one of the darts players said, then donated some of their sandwiches. The landlord picked up her case and she followed, up a dusty, narrow staircase to her room, carrying a plate of sandwiches in one hand while a large martini wobbled in the other.

'This is it,' the landlord said and deposited her case on the floor. 'I'll leave you to it then. If there's anything you want, I'll be in the bar 'til quite late,' he added, as he closed the door on his way out.

Jenny felt exhausted. The room was tiny. A single bed, a small hand painted cupboard and a washbasin struggled with her body, and her case, for the available space. Intermittent cheers from the darts match below reverberated up through the rafters. She sat on the bed, sipped at the martini and tucked into the sandwiches. She hadn't a clue where she was. The map was still in the car and no way was she going back downstairs, through that lot, to fetch it. Opening the small window allowed the sound of the sea to compete with the noises from below. The input of air was like nectar. She gulped at its freshness for many minutes, before organising herself for sleep, which came like a knockout blow.

In the morning Owen Parry, the landlord of the Ship Inn, shuffled around her serving breakfast in the bar. Of medium height, with a balding head and a bulging waistline, he wore a fawn cardigan over a grey polo neck shirt. While he brought toast, bacon, eggs and coffee, they talked.

'If it's walking you want,' he said in response to her enquiry, 'the coastal path begins by the sea wall.'

'I may be back tonight. Can I leave the car?' she asked.

'Very good,' he replied. 'The car will be fine where it is.'

Outside, afterwards, in the square, the day was bright, the wind whipped across her cheeks. Beyond the sea wall was a bay and she watched the sun glint on the breakers as they rolled ashore. She could see the coastal path Owen Parry had mentioned, winding its way along the edge of the dunes.

Without warning, from off the beach, a man appeared from behind the sea wall. He made her jump. She hadn't noticed him approach. A white baseball cap, pulled well down, hid most of his face and a red anorak covered his body. Jenny tried a smiled, but he looked away. For a second she felt her body tremble. He passed by without saying a word.

She turned and watched his hunched figure lope across the grassy square towards the shop. Needing chocolate and a drink for her walk, she followed on behind.

The door stuck a little when she pushed on it. A fluttery bell gonged above her head and she giggled. The man with the white baseball cap was talking to the woman behind the counter. When she approached they stopped and he stood aside. Again she tried a smile, but his stubbled face looked away.

She picked up a Mars bar, some crisps, and a small bottle of Lucozade. The man moved further away when she reached across him for the crisps.

'How long would it take, along the coastal path, to get to the next village?' she asked the woman, when she handed over her purchases.

'Oh, I don't know,' the woman replied. There was a hint of a Birmingham accent. 'John you're a walker. How long would you say?'

'About three to four hours,' he replied. He spoke in a gruff disinterested tone and kept his head down, looking at a newspaper. 'It's not that far, just lots of ups and downs,' he added as an afterthought.

There was something familiar about his accent. She couldn't put a tag on it, his off-putting demeanour threw up too much of a defensive wall. But in his dialect there was a mixture of things she'd heard before. And for some strange reason he made her nervous, so she quickly headed for the door. The two of them began talking again as she pulled it closed.

Jenny was sitting on the bench by the harbour wall, studying her map, when the same man walked quietly past her and back onto the beach. That strange tingling sensation, like a small electric shock, passed through her body again. Why, she thought, and wondered if her nervous system was still on edge from the events of the other week. She watched the man's hunched figure stride across the bay. The wind off the sea cut through her pullover and she shivered, it was time to get moving.

There were a few fluffy clouds scudding across in the fresh breeze, but the sky was predominately blue. On the coastal path she was able to pace out briskly. The man in the red anorak was still walking across the sand, in front of her. When he reached the end of the bay he cut inshore, clambered over some rocks, and disappeared.

The coastal path meandered up and down like a switch-back. Breathlessly reaching each mini summit, her reward was a vista of spectacular proportions, before descending, helter-skelter and sometimes leglessly out of control, down into endless perfect havens of enchanting rock and water. Not a soul crossed her path all morning. London and the problems there seemed like a distant planet.

The village of her destination wasn't really a village at all, not even a hamlet. A farm, a few holiday bungalows and a small cottage on the sea front that offered tea and toasted sandwiches on the lawn, was about it. There, she rested her legs and enjoyed the view. While sipping tea, she thought about the man with the white baseball cap. Suddenly she recalled the accent. Somewhere in the deep structures of his vowels and consonants was a North Wales/Lancashire dialect. It was hidden, masked by a blanket of sophistication. But the hard nuances were still there. Living away from home she'd forgotten the sounds.

On the way back her mind played with the idea. The man she'd seen in the shop had the appearance of an inshore fisherman; a haulier of lobster pots perhaps? But there was something in the voice that didn't match any of those presumptions. No, it couldn't possibly be, she thought. Desperately she tried to recall the glossy photographs in the publicity file. Then she remembered her words to Imogen Quaith. Casper Watkins would go to ground in a place where nobody would think of looking, she had said. She lifted her eyes to take in the coastline and yes, this wild desolate bay could just be that place.

Owen Parry was listening to the football results on the radio when she got back to the Ship Inn. A few other men, some with dogs at their feet, some puffing on pipes or cigarettes, were sitting at tables, with pints of beer, listening as well. The air was thick with tobacco smoke, a coal fire glowed in the corner.

'You made it then,' Parry said when she approached. He didn't really want an answer, his mind was focused on Nationwide League Division Two. She ordered a lager and could feel all the men watching her.

'I think I'll stay another night, if you still have the room.'

'Very good,' he replied.

Minutes later, when the announcer started on the Scottish results, he asked, 'Will you be wanting a meal?'

'Yes please.'

Upstairs in her room, she washed and changed. Using the tiny hand-basin was an exercise in logistics, but afterwards she felt better and was back in the bar by six. The men were gone. Only the remnants of their tobacco smoke remained. The fire, which had been stoked, spat out bits of cinder through a metal guard.

'The wife has nearly finished,' Owen Parry said when he saw her, then disappeared into the kitchen. 'It was a grand day for a walk,' he commented, when he reappeared with a large white plate, overflowing with scampi and chips. She was ravenous and nothing had smelt so good in weeks.

'What a coastline,' she said. 'Tell me Mr Parry, is there a man named John Casper Watkins living in these parts? He's a writer.'

'Not that I know of.'

'He's someone I used to know in London. There was a man in the square today who looked a bit like him. But he was wearing a cap and I couldn't see his face properly. Only wondered.'

'He doesn't come in here anyway. You could ask some of the locals tonight. They'll know. Everybody knows everybody round here. Would you like some vinegar?'

An evening sky of clarity peculiar to the west coast, with reds and pinks at the horizon induced Jenny to explore the surrounding countryside. Deciding to take the car, her idea was to try and find a way down to the headland, where she'd seen the man on the beach disappear. About half a mile from the village there was a lane off to the right that seemed to head that way. It was about another mile before it tapered off into a single un-weeded track, shrouded with overhanging trees. She stopped the car, got out and listened. A tree rustled in the breeze, occasionally a bird sang, but nothing else moved or stirred. The track became narrow. Her skills at reversing weren't that good, so she ventured no further.

The church clock chimed ten when she parked the car by the pub. The Norman Tower was prominent in the clear night sky. She walked down to the sea wall, lent against its structure, took deep breaths and watched the whiteness of the breakers as they rolled in. Then, as though from nowhere, the man with the white baseball cap again appeared around the wall. He took her by surprise and made her jump. He hadn't seen her either and they nearly collided.

'Mister Watkins?' she asked. He couldn't have heard, so she asked again.

'Mister Casper Watkins?' she repeated. He still didn't reply, just tucked his chin into his collar and kept moving.

She watched his hunched body weave across the square. Then, like a ghost in the night, he vanished, somewhere behind the shop; one moment he'd been there, the next gone.

The bar in the Ship Inn was busy. A different crowd that night. A Saturday night crowd; husbands and wives, tourists, walkers, people off boats. More her sort of people. She felt relaxed and engaged in conversation with a group from Blackpool; their boat was anchored in the bay.

'Morlais might know of your Mister Watkins,' Owen Parry said, when she purchased some drinks. He pointed to a small, neat, dark haired man, wearing a Fair Isle sweater, at the end of the bar.

'Morlais used to be the relief postman until his eyes went,' Owen Parry added. 'Couldn't read the addresses anymore,' he chuckled. 'Morlais. A minute please,' he called out and beckoned with his arm. The man ambled over.

'This lady is looking for a friend of hers,' Owen Parry said. 'A writer I think?' he added.

'That's right,' Jenny said. 'Name of John Casper Watkins. He used to live in London. I haven't seen him in years, but I thought I spotted him in the square today.'

'H'm. Wouldn't know for sure,' Morlais replied, scratching his chin. 'There's a funny bloke, who never talks to anybody, living at the end of the bay in Mary Mcquillam's old cottage,' he said, continuing to scratch. 'Mind you, everybody who's ever lived there has been slightly daft. I don't know if his name is Watkins though. She'd probably know at the Post Office. There was a hell of a kerfuffle once when his mail went astray. He has it delivered there now.'

Next morning, before breakfast, Jenny sat at the tiny window of her bedroom, watching the square. The church clock was chiming eight. She wanted to see if the man with the white baseball cap would reappear. For half an hour she waited, but nothing moved, until a van hurtled down the hill and screeched to a halt outside the shop. The driver threw tied up bundles of newspapers into the doorway, then revved away again, leaving a cloud of diesel fumes in the air. In time, wearing a blue tracksuit, the woman from the shop emerged and struggled with the bundles. Jenny put on her anorak. Outside, the vivid colours of yesterday had disappeared. Rain was in the air, grey prevailed in the sky and the temperature had dropped at least five degrees. When she reached the shop, the woman was still struggling with the bundles of newspapers. Jenny helped carry one in.

'That's kind of you,' Katherine Walker said. She began cutting the string around the bundles.

'I'll take an Observer when you find one, please,' Jenny said.

'I don't know why they tie them in such knots,' Katherine Walker replied. 'Rips my hands to pieces. Ah, Observers at last. They never send enough.'

'I've been trying to trace an old acquaintance,' Jenny said, handing over the money for the newspaper. 'He's someone my parents knew in North Wales. They told me he lived around here; name of Casper Watkins. In the pub they mentioned you might know. Somebody said he could be living at Mary Macquillam's old cottage, at the end of the bay?'

Katherine Walker stopped counting out the change and looked up at her.

'There's a John Watkins living there. Don't know about Casper,' she replied, then continued doling out the change. 'You were in yesterday weren't you?'

'That's right. Early in the morning.'

'Well John Watkins was standing next to you then.'

'Oh well, it must be somebody else,' Jenny said. 'Perhaps they got the names mixed up. Thanks anyway.' She headed for the door.

'From North Wales, you said?' Katherine Walker called out as she was about to pull it closed.

'Yes, but it was a long time ago. I hardly knew him.' The bell gonged as the door shut.

The Parry's were just about up by the time Jenny got back to the Ship Inn. Sunday in West Wales is a time of peaceful repose. Jenny had read half the newspaper before breakfast appeared.

'I think I'll explore the beach this morning Mister Parry,' she said when he eventually brought the toast. 'Is it all right to leave the car?'

'Yes it'll be fine. Nothing much moves around here on a Sunday.'

'I want to try and find the man I was telling you about. The lady at the shop seems to think he may live at that cottage at the end of the bay. Is there a way up from the beach?'

'If the tide's out you may be able to scramble up over the rocks. You'll have to be careful though, it runs quite fast down there. When the tide's in, the only way back is along a lane that links up with the coastal path.'

'I think I'll give it a try. If I'm not back by dark, you'd better send out a search party.'

'Very good,' he said and then disappeared into the kitchen.

Walking across the bay she wondered why she was continuing to dabble in all this. Her fingers had already been burnt prying into other peoples business. What was she trying to prove?

It took about twenty minutes to reach the rocks at the far end. Years of pounding sea water had made the boulders slippery, like ice. She continually missed her footing. Then, brambles and gorse snagged at her clothes, but gradually a rough track appeared where the undergrowth had been flattened by regular use.

A hedge confronted her; she found a gap through which she could see a dry stone wall. Behind it was a cottage, built of similar material. She stopped and told herself she could quit this nonsense there and then. She could go back to the pub and forget the whole thing. Leave, knowing she may have spotted Casper Watkins. Perhaps pass the information onto Anthony Rathenberg and let somebody else follow it up. She wasn't paid to involve herself and it obviously wasn't appreciated.

Quietly, she crawled through the hedge and lent on the wall. The cottage was tiny. It looked a mess of cracked plaster and rotting window frames. Surely, Casper Watkins couldn't live here, not after Ebury Terrace.

To try and get a better look she heaved herself up on the wall. In doing so she dislodged a stone. It rolled off the top on to a pile of boulders on the other side and made a cracking sound when it landed.

The noise disturbed the man. He had been earthing up seed potatoes on the far side of the cottage and came to investigate. She was going to run away but a bramble impaired her movement.

'Can I ask you what you're doing?' the man shouted.

Jenny gulped. The stubbled face she had seen yesterday was only feet away, glaring at her.

'I'm sorry, I was looking for a Mister Watkins. I was told he lived here.'

'This is private land, you're trespassing, I must ask you to leave.' He was scowling.

'All right, I'll leave. Only the other week, I was visiting some friends in Gwernaffield and they mentioned that John Watkins' mother was very ill. They said he didn't know. They said they'd tried to trace him, but he couldn't be found anywhere.' Emotion edged her words.

'What right have you to come here. What's your name? You're not from the papers are you? If you are I'll call the police,' he said. The phrases fired at her like bullets from a machine gun. He was standing very close. His eyes flared, he'd been holding a spade and waved it in the air threateningly. She was frightened.

'All right I'm going. My name is Jenny Millington and I'm not from the papers, but I'm sure you're Casper Watkins. I promise you, your mother is very ill. She needs you, please believe me. And your friend Henson is dead. He's been murdered. I was in your flat last week and found his body.' Tears began to tumble down her cheeks. The wind off the sea blew them into the air.

She stepped back.

'I'll go now,' she said, still sobbing. 'But I thought you should know, that's all.' Her body was shaking. She began to move, but the brambles snagged again at her feet and clothes.

'What do you mean Henson's dead?' he called after her.

'He was murdered in your apartment,' she blubbered through more tears. 'I was supposed to meet him there, on business. It's been in the newspapers. Read it if you don't believe me.'

'Who the hell are you?' he growled.

CHAPTER

AFTER SHE HAD GONE HE SAT FOR A LONG TIME BY THE FIRE TRYING to comprehend everything she'd told him. Her business card was in his hand and he re-read it over and over. In all his dealings with Knott and Pearson he'd never come across her name before.

In the garden, when he first saw her, he'd been confused. She'd rolled off so many details about his personal life, he really thought it was a set-up. However, what she said had astonished him. There'd been no alternative but to invite her in. Sitting across the table from her, listening to her passionate words, watching her blonde hair, her blue eyes, the creamy complexion, the way her mouth seemed to curl when she emphasised something, had riveted his attention

To learn his dear friend Henson was no longer alive was inconceivable. To know he'd been murdered in such a brutal way was staggering; they had been chums for over thirty years. And his mother. She'd never needed him for anything, but when she did, he hadn't been there and now he was distraught with guilt.

Once the girl had calmed down, he'd managed to coax out a few more details. Initially, she'd been reluctant to elaborate. The events at Ebury Terrace obviously still evoked pain, clearly she was upset. Huge droplets of tears had rolled down her cheeks as she recounted the gory details. But by the time she'd finished, she'd told it all. He'd watched her closely, only occasionally interrupting with a prompt, and when it was all out they'd suddenly seemed very close; like confidants, almost like lovers; a secret shared, about which only they knew the truth.

Alone, on his green settee, he looked around. The room was a mess. Half read newspapers were scattered everywhere, pullovers dangled on the backs of chairs, dust and crumbs littered the floor. What must the girl have thought, he mused.

She had also mentioned something about Knott and Pearson withholding his royalties. Living at the cottage, money was a commodity that had become almost irrelevant. He'd left the trappings of life behind in London. Apart from rent, booze and food, there wasn't much else he required down here and when he wanted money Katherine would always cash him a cheque. Everything else he'd left for Henson to deal with. There was an arrangement with his bank to transfer funds from his business account, whenever his personal account got low. When the royalties came in, Henson took his commission, paid the bills, then any surplus was invested on the money market. By Caspers' own rough estimate, there should have been about a million pounds in savings swilling around somewhere.

Lately, he'd developed a habit of throwing his mail, unopened, into the recess of the window by the cottage door. Until his writing was back on track the outside world could go to hell, he'd stipulated one day. He had to fish around amongst the clutter to find his most recent bank statement. Then a cold horror hit him. The balance showing was down to just over a thousand pounds. Frantically he searched for the other statements. On all of them only debits were registered. No transfers of credit were recorded anywhere.

'Hell,' he cursed and kicked at the pile of accumulated mail at his feet. 'Bloody hell,' he repeated and kicked out again.

He slumped in the settee with the statements in his hand and stared at the fire. A faint aroma of the girl's perfume lingered on the furniture. He could still visualise her face and the way her body wriggled with embarrassment. 'Bloody hell and damnation,' he said once more.

For hours he sat motionless on that settee, thinking, planning, reminiscing, spasmodically dozing into a light sleep. By the time dawn crept up, he was still on the settee, but he'd made up his mind to go back. There was a lot to sort out which couldn't be done from the cottage.

A mini bus took him to Pembroke Dock. Then a train to Swansea and from there, straight through to Paddington. Travelling light, with just a holdall, he returned as he had set out, unnoticed and unannounced.

An odour of must greeted him when he opened the door at Ebury Terrace. A cobweb brushed his face as he walked in. The lounge looked untidy. Chairs were askew, scraps of paper and other materials lay on the carpet. Mrs Hart, his cleaner, obviously hadn't been. Dust covered the clear areas of his desk. Mail was strewn across the rest, all of it opened. In the middle, held down by his glass paperweight, was a sheet of note-paper, headed by the logo of the Metropolitan Police and addressed to him. Back sloping hand writing told him they held Henson's set of keys, and he was to contact them upon his return. The note said they had removed all the bedding from the main bedroom and the towels and mats from the bathroom. A list of everything taken was on a separate sheet. Both sheets were signed by an Inspector John Palmer. There was no tape in his answer phone when he tried to replay it.

Slowly he walked around. The furniture was all in tact, the carpets, the pictures, the drapes were all in place, yet somehow it felt as though the room had been violated. Hesitatingly he moved towards the master bedroom. The girl's description of her findings had been graphic. He still couldn't comprehend what Henson had been up to.

The door was ajar. It didn't look like his room anymore. The bed was stripped, the drapes and the mattress gone. In the bathroom blood stains streaked the floor and bath. A rancid smell hung in the air.

Feeling nauseated he moved away, he'd seen enough. As he closed the bedroom door he noticed his figurine, his prize in New York, for 'Flame in the Sky', wasn't on the bedside table.

In the lounge he checked the police list. It wasn't listed there either.

The cluttered mess on his desk annoyed him. He was about to sweep it all off with one dramatic gesture of his hand, but a piece of paper sticking out from under his word processor halted the impulse. He switched on the desk lamp, lifted the word processor and found a copy of his business account bank statement underneath. It must have got caught under there. His hand trembled when he saw five withdrawals, each for one hundred thousand pounds. And, before those transactions, half a million had also been transferred in from his money market account. No way had he authorised any of that. He searched the desk drawer for the cheque book, but it wasn't there.

Confused, he slumped into his leather back, swivel, writing chair. What on earth has Henson been up to, he wondered. At the cottage, in amongst his mail on the window ledge, he recalled seeing two letters from Henson asking him to get in touch, regarding a business deal. There had also been another couple from his bank, requiring him to contact them about large withdrawals. He found his cheque book listed on the police schedule, as well as copies of his bank statements. The one in his hand must have come adrift or been missed in the melee Jenny Millington described. The figurine though, was definitely not on the list.

He decided to lie low until morning. Settling down for the night, in the spare bedroom, he found Jenny Millington's business card when he unpacked his holdall.

CHAPTER

'MISS MILLINGTON?' SHE HEARD A VOICE SAY WHEN SHE ANSWERED the phone on her desk. It was another one of those busy days when it had never stopped ringing.

'That's right,' she replied. It was nearing five o'clock and she hadn't paid much attention to the voice.

'Miss Millington, it's Casper Watkins. Is it all right to speak?'

His voice and the mention of his name momentarily stunned her into silence. Surreptitiously, she glanced around the office, hoping no-one had heard. Before leaving his cottage last Sunday she'd promised not to reveal to her firm his whereabouts for two weeks. 'I need time to sort all this out, my way,' he had said, after she had answered all his questions. 'Please will you give me two weeks,' he'd pleaded, while they sat in front of the fire together on the green settee, drinking tea. 'I swear to you, I know nothing about Henson's death. I'll go to the police when I get back, but I want it kept quiet. If your employers have not heard from me in two weeks, then you can say where I am, but I must have time to try and get to the bottom of all this. Henson was my friend.'

Maybe it was the pleading in his eyes, maybe it was the emotional chord in his voice when he said Henson's name, but for some inexplicable reason she agreed. He could have been lying. For all she knew he may have been involved with the murder, but the distraught look on his face, as she recounted the events at Ebury Terrace, said something different. If she hadn't read all his books she might not have agreed. But in all his stories there was an underlying element of decency. Beneath the involved hyperbole of his plots, there was always a search for the truth and a moral conclusion. So she agreed to give him two weeks, but she never expected to hear from him again.

'Miss Millington,' the voice on the phone repeated.

'Yes, I am sorry, you took me by surprise.'

'Miss Millington, I apologise for bothering you, but I wonder if I could see you?'

The very thought of meeting up with him again set her pulse racing.

'Where are you?' she said, hearing her heartbeat thumping in her chest.

'I'm in a phone box, about two blocks away from your office. There's a pub opposite called the Duke of Wellington. Do you know it?'

'Yes.'

'Can I meet you there in half an hour?'

She didn't know what to say. He spoke again.

'I've still got the beard and the baseball cap. I don't want anybody to recognise me. Do you think my disguise will hold?' She detected a hint of humour in his voice. 'Oh and by the way I've been to the police. You can check with that nasty Inspector Palmer if you wish. Like you, I'm now on domestic remand, pending further inquiries.'

She almost giggled. 'Well the disguise fooled me,' she said. 'And I don't think anybody from here will go to that pub. It's too scruffy for any of this lot. Half an hour you said?'

'Thanks,' he replied and rang off.

Oh dear, she thought, here I go again.

The Duke of Wellington was a rundown watering hole used by the men on the building site across the road. A gaggle of them, in dust covered jeans and T-shirts, were gathered around the bar when she arrived. Sitting in the corner, with his stubbled face half covered by the Evening Standard, wearing an oversized red pullover and a pair of blue jeans, he could have been one of them; a jobbing carpenter perhaps?

The men's heads all turned when she walked over to him. That tingling sensation was back in her body again. If only Imogen Quaith and the people at the office could see me now, she thought.

'Thanks for coming. What'll you have?' he said, getting up from his seat.

'Oh, a large vodka and tonic please.'

At the cottage he'd looked diffident, almost gaunt. It may have been a trick of the light but in the hurly-burly of a London pub he seemed more at ease, almost relaxed. There was warmth in his expression when he looked at her.

'I hope that's all right,' he said when he put the drink down on the table beside her. 'If you want some more lemon, please let me know.'

'That's fine,' she said after a sip. Her body was shaking. She hoped it didn't show and prayed the vodka would settle her nerves.

'Firstly I must apologise for my rudeness on Sunday,' he said, then supped at the large goblet of red wine in front of him. 'You see I escaped to West Wales, basically to avoid people. I'd been having a barren time with my writing and needed somewhere quiet to get my head down and concentrate.'

'Has it worked?' she asked.

He hesitated before replying. She thought he really had quite a kind face underneath its mask of obduracy.

'To a limited degree,' he replied.

'Have you started on something?'

'Sort of.'

'Can I ask what?' she said.

'You can, but I won't tell you.' Humour was still in his eyes, so she responded.

'Purely professional interest you understand,' she said.

'That's why I won't tell you.' They both sipped at their drinks at the same time. The builders noisily departed, chiding each other as they pushed out through the door. They were now alone except for the barmaid.

'It's just that you told me so much all at once on Sunday,' he began. 'I really didn't have time to take it all in and at first I didn't really believe you. I mean, I don't know anything about you and you kept dealing out all these personal details about my life. I was convinced you were from the press.'

'Well now you know I'm not.'

'Yes and I'm very grateful to you, for everything.' His brown eyes sparkled. 'There's so much to sort out. I just need a bit more information before I begin.' He paused for another sup of his wine. 'First, I've got to organise poor Henson's things. He had nobody you know. Like me he was an only child.' He hesitated after he'd said that and looked away. 'And then there's my mother. I must try and get up to North Wales in the next day or so.'

Jenny hadn't mentioned about her meeting with his mother and Trevor. She was going to say something about it, then changed her mind. If she had learnt anything in all this, it was to keep her mouth shut, so she let him do the talking.

'You said that my mother was in hospital,' he said. 'You didn't happen to find out which one did you?'

'Denbigh.'

'Oh you are an angel.' She guessed he could be quite a charmer when required.

'Princess Margaret Ward,' Jenny added.

His face beamed. She felt her body tingle and gulped at the vodka.

'You wouldn't come and work for me would you? I think I'd do better with someone like you around, especially now Henson's gone.'

'If you don't come up with a new book soon, I might take you up on the offer. Things are pretty grim in publishing.'

'Surely not. There's never been so much publicity about books. When I started you were lucky if you got a mention in one of the quality papers.'

'Publicity's all very well, it's sales we need. Competition's hot. When this fortnight's up is there any crumb of comfort I can offer my employers?'

He winced and for a second his face tightened. The gaunt look almost returned but she could see him fight it off with a false smile.

'I've started on something about a Royal scandal and a plot to convert Britain into a Republic, with machinations over the Euro. It's got some good bits but I haven't got it right yet,' he lied.

She wondered.

'Well accountants rule the roost these days,' she said. 'At Knott and Pearson profit margin is now the King. The bottom line they call it. For every penny they spend, they expect a pound of flesh.'

'Is that so. Let me get you another drink.'

She sat back, glad of the break. She was pleased with herself. So far she'd held her own, something those at the office couldn't always claim, when dealing with Casper.

'I don't want to revive bad memories Jenny,' he said when he returned with the drinks. The use of her name made her heart quiver. 'But when you were at the apartment did you notice a bronze figurine on the bedside table?'

For a moment those awful images flooded back into her head. 'Oh gosh I don't know. Everything became such a blur. It was horrible. All I can remember is Henson's crumpled body in the bath.' Her voice tightened with each word.

'Of course, of course, it was inconsiderate of me to ask. You had to endure enough of all that with the police.' His hand touched her arm in a gesture of apology.

'Was it important?' she asked. Their eyes met and held each others gaze.

'Not particularly in terms of value. It was a literary prize I was awarded in New York. But it's gone. The police removed lots of things but not that.'

'Perhaps Henson took it?'

'No, he hated it, called it my gong.'

She realised he was staring at her. 'You know you have the most extraordinarily pretty face,' he said 'The way your hair frames it and the colouring in your eyes makes it very photogenic.'

She giggled with embarrassment 'Come on Casper, I bet you say that to all the girls.'

'No I mean it. Photography used to be a hobby. When I worked on the Rhyl Journal I took all the pictures that went with my articles. You had to do everything in those days. I was quite good.'

She smiled and subconsciously angled her head to one side as though she was posing. She hadn't realised she was doing it until he spoke again.

'There you are. That's it, perfect,' he said and joined his thumbs and forefingers together in an imaginary frame. She realised he was flirting with her and felt self conscious. His hand touched her arm again. ' I could show you if you like. I've got lots of my old prints at the apartment.'

She laughed. 'Come up and see my etchings you mean.'

His eyes were smiling again.

At that moment a crowd of office revellers came into the bar. Their noisy joviality broke the moment. She sat back in her seat, relieved to have an intervention. He continued to sit forward with his eyes focused on her face.

'The apartment's only a few stops away on the underground. We could go there now, if you were interested,' he said.

'No Casper, I don't think so. I really haven't recovered from my last visit there yet. Not tonight, honestly.'

'Well perhaps I could treat you to a meal? It's the least I can do after all your help.'

'It's very kind of you, but there's some work I have to catch up on. Thanks all the same.'

'Well another time perhaps?' he asked.

'Yes, maybe another time?'

In bed, snuggled up in her duvet, she could still visualise his face. On Sunday he'd been awkward, intimidating. Now, having seen the traces of humour around his eyes, she felt completely different. Smitten wasn't quite the right word, fascinated would be more exact.

CHAPTER

THE SIGHT OF HIS MOTHER'S HOLLOW CHEEKED FACE WHEN HE WALKED into her hospital ward was a shock. The vitality he'd known all his life had gone, leaving only an ashen shell. Her arms were like matchsticks. A blank stare greeted him.

'Mother,' he said as he moved in closer.

'John,' she replied in a faint whisper. The muscles on her face couldn't cope with a smile. A puffing of the cheeks was all that was possible.

'Mother,' he repeated, and held out his hand.

'You were able to come then son?' she said, clutching on to his hand.

'Of course I was able to come mother. If I had known before I would have been here all the time.' Her hand felt tiny in his muscular grip.

'You're always so busy son and we couldn't find you.' A panting breath accompanied every word.

'I know mother. But I'm never too busy to see you. I've been away, trying to write. Sort of self imposed purdah I suppose.'

'Oh John you're always up to something.' A hint of humour forced it's way into her breathless voice.

'Well I'm here now. We've got to get you fit and out of this place. I've spoken to the doctor. He says you're doing well.'

'Well, I don't know about well. They've stopped the pain, thank God.'

'You can do it mother. I've never known you ill in all my life. This isn't going to beat you. I'm here now. I'll see to that.'

'Oh John, you do make me laugh.'

'That's the spirit mother. What about Trevor? Where's he?'

'John I've been so worried. He's had to go back into the home. He'd been getting along fine at the cottage.'

'We'll sort something out. You're not to worry. Leave it all to me.'

To gain access to 'Cartref' Casper had to confront Iris Francis. He'd lost his key some years ago. Her greeting was taciturn.

'I've run the hoover around,' she said, as she opened the front door and stood aside. A smell of fresh furniture polish hit Casper's nostrils. The brasses gleamed, the black surround of the fireplace shone like a mirror, the furniture was all arranged tidily. Iris Francis's heart of gold was tempered by a streak of indispensability and that had been their pique for years. When he was young, if his mother was out or away, she would always cook him a meal or ask him in for tea. Usually he was quite happy to be alone.

Originally he was going to stay at the Hanbury Arms, in the village. Economies were now necessary and he'd managed quite adequately in West Wales and, 'Cartref', after all, was his home.

The doctor at the hospital had said it would be some weeks before his mother could be moved. 'Even then she probably won't be able to cope at home. Her age is against it.' So, for the time being, he decided 'Cartref' would be his base.

After West Wales he found London very noisy, aggressive and unfriendly. His meeting with John Palmer had been particularly unpleasant. With the benefit of hindsight he should have consulted his Solicitor first and taken him along. That bastard Palmer had virtually accused him of Henson's murder. They'd made him take a DNA test and give fingerprints. 'We have the authority to hold you,' Palmer had said. 'There is sufficient motive.' He was referring of course to the missing money.

Palmer had it all written out on a schedule. In addition to the half million, Henson had also drawn two cheques of ten thousand pounds, payable to someone by the name of Laidlaw. Those cheques had been paid into a bank account in Fulham, which was subsequently closed.

'Drug money, I expect,' Palmer said sarcastically. 'A typical drug money laundering operation,' he sneered.

'What are you doing about it?' Casper asked.

'We'll see if we can get an address for this man Laidlaw from the bank. It'll probably be fictitious though.'

The half million pounds Henson drew in cash was taken in five separate lots of a hundred thousand. Casper had phoned his bank about it. They told him Henson said it was needed for a film project. The bank did wonder and wrote to him, but the letters had remained unopened on the ledge of the window recess, in West Wales.

'When can I have my bank statements back?' Casper asked Palmer.

'When all our initial inquiries are complete.'

'What about my agent's body? I want to arrange a funeral.'

'Our forensic tests must be finished first.'

'You guys certainly take your time.'

'We haven't completely eliminated you from our enquiries,' Palmer continued as their meeting wound up. 'We'll need to see you again,' he added.

'Next time my solicitor will be present,' Casper had retorted.

'That's your prerogative,' Palmer said with a shrug of his shoulders.

Geoffrey Appleby had represented Casper in legal matters for many years. He was a crusty old stick, with a droll sense of humour, but Casper had always trusted him. They were sitting across an untidy, deed cluttered desk in the solicitor's Lincoln's Inn office. An aroma of pipe tobacco tainted the air.

'I can put a private investigator onto this, if you want?' Appleby had said when Casper explained about the missing money.

'No, complete waste of time,' Casper replied. 'I haven't a clue what the silly old sod has done with it, but whatever it is, I hope he enjoyed himself. Anyway you can't sue a dead man.'

'I'm surprised you gave him authority to draw such an amount,' Appleby said. His bushy eyebrows fluttered in a gesture of incredulity.

'I trusted him implicitly. When I first came to London he virtually supported me until the royalties for my first book came through. In those days, of course, in money terms, we were talking about peanuts, so there wasn't really a necessity to put a limit on it. 'Flame in the Sky' changed all that. But I'd still guarantee his honesty.'

'Well, you're not so wealthy now,' Appleby said.

The bank had supplied Casper with copies of his bank statements. Appleby had them in front of him and jotted down some figures on a loose piece of paper before he spoke again.

'H'm,' he began. 'You're not exactly broke, but all things added together, I would say there's about two hundred thousand left. But you've got the lease on the apartment to pay and the repayments on the Ferrari, so it's not going to last for ever.'

'Those buggers at Knott and Pearson owe me royalties Geoff, they stopped paying me when I disappeared. What can you do about that?'

'I'll write to them but you're under contract to write another book. They're probably within their rights to hold something back.'

'I just need a bit of time Geoff. See what you can do old chap.'

Sitting in his mother's armchair, in front of the fire at 'Cartref', he suddenly felt very lonely. Henson had been his only real friend in the world, the only one he could call on in a crisis like this. He'd asked Palmer if he could go to Henson's house in Kensington. He was sure there'd be a clue there, to the whereabouts of his missing money.

'We've sealed the place off for the time being,' Palmer had said. 'It's out of bounds until we have a definite motive for his murder.'

Casper knew his way around Henson's study. His agent was always mislaying things and together they'd acquired a comic ritual in looking for them. Usually, it involved trying to get Henson to remember the last thing he'd done before taking his daily fix. Like kids they'd laugh as they attempted to retrace his actions.

He was certainly going to miss him. The money wasn't important. Considering where they both came from, it had been acquired rather easily. He just couldn't believe his old friend would cheat on him. He knew then that somehow or another he had to get into that study.

CHAPTER

THE FICTION DEPARTMENT AT KNOTT AND PEARSON WAS UNDER pressure. Pressure from above and pressure from within. Memos were circulated almost daily, by management, regarding the poor sales figures and the need for rapid improvement. Nerve ends became stretched, tempers flared, they were working to a deadline. Two new novels had to be finalised by the end of the month. And Imogen was at her bitchy worst. News of Jenny's lunch date with Anthony Rathenberg had somehow leaked out, and the police had been in contact many times about Henson's murder. Not being the centre of attention for once, evoked a vein of jealousy in Imogen that stood out like a carbuncle.

'You'll have to work on late,' she lectured to Jenny one morning. 'The Mchugh novel has got to be ready by the twenty-eighth.'

'That shouldn't be a problem,' Jenny replied. 'I've always worked late when something needed doing.'

'Well I'm just telling you, in case you have any fancy ideas about gallivanting off on one of your jaunts.'

Jenny held her tongue. Sometimes, by not responding to Imogen's vitriol she could gain a moral victory. She was never going to win any slanging match with Imogen. The woman became so argumentative, and she could shout louder. In the middle of all this mayhem the phone rang on Jenny's desk. At the time she was photocopying on the other side of the room. Imogen was near to her phone and picked up the receiver.

'It's for you,' she hectored, then banged the phone down on the desk and stormed off to her room, like a prima donna, who had been overlooked for a lead part.

'Hello,' Jenny said tentatively.

'Who was that?' Anthony Rathenberg said.

'Oh Imogen, in one of her moods,' Jenny replied.

'Gosh, I didn't recognise her,' Anthony Rathenberg said. 'Jenny, I've got two tickets for the Royal Opera House tomorrow night. The Royal Ballet are doing 'Nutcracker'. My mother and father are coming up from Sussex. It's one of his favourites and he would like to meet you. This Casper Watkins affair was his hobby horse 'til he lumbered me with it. Can you make it?'

Jenny was gobsmacked.

'Tony I'd love to come. Trouble is we're on overtime with the Mchugh novel and Imogen has imposed a three line whip until it's completed.'

'Don't worry about that. One evening isn't going to matter. You leave that to me. You'll come then?'

'Well, yes please, if you think it'll be all right.'

'Good. I'll pick you up at your flat, about seven, if that's OK. I'll speak with Imogen.'

'Thank you very much Tony,' she said.

As soon as she replaced the receiver the doubts flooded in. When Imogen found out, hell would have no fury like it. And how did Anthony Rathenberg know her address? Fortunately she was far too busy to dwell on any of it for long.

For the remainder of the day Imogen remained in her room. Normally, if she wanted something, she would come out into the general office and get it herself, but that day she buzzed through on the phone, for one of the juniors to fetch everything she required. At lunchtime she disappeared and was gone for more than three hours.

'Brandy fumes are tainting an already tense atmosphere,' the junior who had to answer one of her many calls told Jenny, jokingly, later in the afternoon.

At five o'clock she emerged from her room. 'I'm going upstairs now for an Editor's meeting and I shan't be back. I hope everything here will be cleared up before you all go,' she hollered and stomped out. The others all looked at each other and smiled.

That evening Jenny worked on until nine. When she'd finished they were two days ahead on the Mchugh novel. Only the artwork needed completing and that was out of her control.

Sitting on the tube next morning, anticipating another difficult day, something at the bottom of the showbiz page in the newspaper caught her attention. Filming on the new Karponti-Di Angello movie had ground to a halt, the footnote stated. A problem with funding was given as the reason. She read it over a couple of times, then remembered a conversation with John Palmer at Kensington Police Station. He'd called her in again after her weekend in North Wales.

'You are supposed to report in if you have been out of the district,' he'd said, when she'd arrived.

The interview turned out to be an unpleasant and uncomfortable experience. It seemed Palmer's real purpose for calling her in, was to go over her evidence, in case she had forgotten something. For Jenny, the memory of those awful moments still cut deep. Having to relive them again in front of Palmer was painful. For most of the interview he either paced the room or stood over her, posturing like a belligerent school teacher.

'I've told you all this before,' she cried out in anguish, somewhere in the middle of his interrogation. 'You've got my statement. If you want any more I'll have to consult my solicitor. You said this meeting was going to be about me not reporting in.'

He eased up a little after that, but later on, he asked, 'Did Littlewood mention anything to you about money when you met up?' He was standing over her at the time in his shirt sleeves; a pair of gaudy red braces and an equally revolting tie of the same colour faced her.

'No, why?'

'Large sums of money have gone missing.' Palmer said.

'Our meeting was not of that nature,' Jenny replied. 'I was only trying to find out where Casper Watkins was.'

'And did you?' he said, staring at her.

'No,' she said dogmatically.

Fortunately, the meeting with Palmer was before she discovered Casper's West Wales hideaway. And at the time her mind was too wound up with the emotional aspects of it all, so she hadn't paid much attention to his question. Money was a variant she hadn't considered in all this. Rattling along on the underground towards Ealing Broadway, however, it suddenly developed a significance.

Maybe Casper was instrumental in Henson's murder after all? If his money was misappropriated there'd certainly be a motive? And why was he hiding in West Wales like a recluse? Surely he had enough money to live in surroundings more desirable than that isolated cottage? And why had he abandoned his mother, especially at her age? Why had he stopped writing? When she'd asked him about a new novel she really hadn't believed his reply. Since working at Knott and Pearson she'd met enough authors to know when a germ of a book was in their heads. You could see it in their eyes, catch it in their enthusiasm. Casper's response had been miles wide of both those marks.

Sitting on that train, as it echoed through another tunnel, she wasn't sure of anything any more. She felt lonely and depressed. Living on her own in London, and under pressure in work, wasn't what she hoped working life was going to be. She'd gone out on a limb over this whole affair and now it was all rebounding in her face, like a nightmare.

In the middle of her speculations, suddenly, and without warning, all the lights in the train went out and it screeched to a standstill. Everything was blacked out. Around her people began to moan, curse, complain. Eight-forty-five on a Thursday morning and their world had stopped. Like rabbits in a warren, with no escape, they remained stationary in darkness for some twenty minutes, until the lights came back on.

'A power failure up the line,' they were informed, without apology. Another twenty minutes elapsed. The train then reversed back to West Acton. There, she had to get a bus and it was ten o'clock before she got into work. Dreading the moment, she inched her head around Imogen's doorway.

'I'm sorry I'm late, the tube broke down. There was a power failure and we had to go back to West Acton.'

'I've given the Susan Barton novel to Angela to finish off,' Imogen said without looking up.

'Imogen, I said the tube broke down. There's no panic on the Barton novel. It's another two weeks before we have to finalise on that.'

'You've got enough on your plate with the Mchugh book. You're behind today and I understand you'll be leaving early tonight, so that's

95

my decision,' Imogen said, still without looking up. She took a long draw on her cigarette and exhaled the smoke out through her nostrils.

'The Mchugh book is finished. I stayed behind last night to complete it. There's only the art work to do, and you told me you were organising that.'

'Well you'll have plenty of time to titivate yourself up for this evening then, won't you.' Imogen said, with her eyes still firmly fixed on the paper in front of her.

Jenny turned away and stalked off towards her desk. She decided there and then that Imogen was a complete bitch. Susan Barton was one of Jenny's new authors, they'd met often and got on well. Her work was crisp and inventive and she had wanted to see it all through to publication.

Her evening at the ballet, therefore, was soured before it began. Any elation she may have felt at watching Anthony Rathenberg's blue Rolls Royce pull up outside her flat, or the tingle of desire she experienced on opening her front door, when he stood outside in his dinner jacket, holding out a dozen roses, was tainted with a feeling of guilt, after Imogen's implied accusations.

Rathenberg was charm personified. He complimented her hair. Her dress, a low cut little black number, he declared 'Stunning! It'll definitely be a head turner.' Her knees trembled when she looked into his eyes as he said it.

Sitting alongside him, feeling the Rolls purr through the streets of London, enjoying his aftershave, listening to his patter, was similarly tainted, like eating a chocolate you had desired all week, then having your taste buds sullied with a cold, she mused to herself.

'Tony, how did you discover my address?' she asked on the way to Covent Garden.

'Personnel. They have their uses,' he said and laughed.

She smiled. Being with him was easy. Just like at lunch, his relaxed conversation kept matters effortlessly flowing.

His parents were friendly and charming and made her feel welcome. His father, Gerald, looked just like Tony. The same hair, only greyer; the same blue eyes, though, if anything more piercing, the same manner, only more avuncular. Tall and wiry, he loped like a leopard when he walked. His wife, Julia was different. Expecting someone astute, domineering and intense, Jenny discovered an auburn haired, warm, bubbly countrywoman, who enjoyed riding, effused over her garden and possessed a laugh of rib-tickling enthusiasm. The whole evening was very jolly, the ballet exquisite.

'Now, you are going to come down at the weekend, aren't you my dear,' Gerald Rathenberg said, over interval drinks. His blue eyes sparkled. 'I've got a gelding you'd look great on. And I want to know all you've found out about that bounder Watkins. He and I had some great nights out when I first published his books.'

'Well there's not much to tell on that,' Jenny said trying to avoid his eyes. 'I'd love to come and ride though, but I haven't done much since I lived in North Wales.'

'Riding's something you never forget,' Julia Rathenberg cut in. 'I didn't ride for fifteen years when I had the children, but it all came back afterwards.'

The time flew by, and all too soon Jenny was sitting beside Rathenberg again, in the Rolls, on the way back to Acton. Unfortunately, throughout the evening there'd been this persistent feeling of playing truant with the head boy, behind the head-mistresses back; and knowing the punishment would be waiting for her in the morning.

'I do hope you will be able to make it at the weekend,' Rathenberg said as the Rolls glided to a halt outside her flat. When he leant towards her, every impulse in her body was shouting yes.

'It sounds wonderful Tony. Of course I'd love to come.'

'Good. I'll pick you up here on Friday evening then.'

'Could I drive down myself? I've got some things to sort out after work. They won't take long but if I don't get them done I'll be in trouble.'

'Of course you can. I'll write out some directions and get my secretary to bring them to you in the morning. Dinner is at eight. If you can be there by half seven it'll help.'

'That'll be super Tony, but whatever you do, don't let Imogen know. She'll go ballistic.'

'Oh dear, why?'

'Female cattiness I'm afraid.'

'H'm.' He touched her arm. 'Jenny I have enjoyed this evening and I look forward to the weekend.'

A multitude of emotions rampaged through her head as she sat down in her flat afterwards. Something about not playing with fire, if you don't want to get burned, prevailed. Anthony Rathenberg wasn't married, but she knew from Imogen that there was a long standing relationship with a woman Solicitor. 'A partner in a big legal firm,' Imogen had patronized. 'She jets all over the world, advising Merchant Bankers on takeovers and mergers. And she's very glamorous,' her editor added.

But Jenny knew Anthony Rathenberg had definitely taken a shine to her. He was very handsome, dashing, charming and so far considerate, and there had been little or no romance in her life for a long time. Nobody important anyway. University socialising had provided a few furtive opportunities. In London, there'd been a couple of one night stands of numbing ordinariness, but nothing to send the ovaries into overdrive for years. And you didn't get anywhere by doing nothing, her father used to say.

The invitation for the weekend, she couldn't refuse. Anthony Rathenberg was her employer. He'd asked her twice and his family had repeated it. To turn them down would be impolite, and put her career in jeopardy. But what his motives were, and how far she was prepared to go to accommodate them, was another matter. She'd rejected his offer of a lift to Sussex, just in case she had to get home by herself.

When Jenny arrived in work on Friday morning, the art work for the Mchugh novel, which over the weeks had gathered around her desk, had been removed to Imogen's room.

'I've asked Angela to give me a hand with it,' Imogen said, standing over her, at Jenny's desk, almost gloating, while sucking on a cigarette at the end of her long holder.

'As the Assistant Editor I thought I might have some sort of say in that,' Jenny retorted. The two women glared at each other.

Angela was a recent recruit from a rival publishing house. They'd never really been work pals, colleagues maybe, but Jenny had been aware of a competitive conflict from the outset.

'I want you to know now Jenny that it's only your University degree that got you that title. Angela has far more experience in publishing than you,' Imogen continued.

'What's that supposed to mean?'

'Nothing,' Imogen said and walked away.

For the rest of that morning Jenny was livid.

Fortunately Imogen wasn't around when Helen Dumas handed Jenny the envelope containing directions to 'Peak House'. Tall, elegant, erudite, Helen had been both secretary and confidante to the Rathenberg family for years. She had been Gerald's secretary, before Anthony took over, and office gossip implied she may have also been the old man's mistress as well. Her classic figure, the tailored appearance and well groomed hair, made the assumption plausible.

'I do hope you have a lovely time,' she said standing alongside Jenny's desk. 'It's such a beautiful spot.'

'Thanks Helen. I'm a bit nervous about it really.'

'No need, they're all charming. You don't have to worry, just enjoy yourself.'

'I'll try not to let the side down. That's a super dress Helen,' Jenny said. 'Where did you get that from?'

Helen was in the middle of explaining, when the phone rang on her desk.

'Jenny, it's Casper,' the voice said. 'I was wondering if I could take you out for a meal tomorrow night? You said you might consider it. I've got something to show you.'

His use of her first name scattered her faculties. For a few moments she was flummoxed.

'Er, I've got somebody with me at the moment. I can't make tomorrow night. I'm away for the weekend.'

'Well it's my new book. I need your advice, professionally that is, but off the record as well, if you know what I mean.'

Helen was still standing alongside. Jenny tried to be circumspect.

'Where are you?' she said.

'At the moment in North Wales, but I'm coming to London tomorrow. It is important, I promise you. I'm at a vital stage in the story.'

She had to swallow hard to avoid saying his name. 'Well the weekend is totally out. I have a commitment, which I have to keep.'

'What about Monday?'

'Monday should be OK. As I said I've got somebody with me at the moment.'

'Oh, all right, I'll telephone you on Monday. Thanks a lot,' he said, and rang off.

Jenny could feel herself getting warm.

'Nice to be popular,' Helen Dumas said.

'I'm not so sure. Sometimes it gets complicated.'

'Enjoy it while you're young,' Helen said and walked away.

CHAPTER

IN WOODED COUNTRY, ABOUT A MILE OFF THE BRIGHTON ROAD, A long, narrow, chipping track led through a tall set of wrought iron gates with a cattle grid. Jenny drove on, ranch style fencing and mature oaks lined the driveway, Friesians were grazing in a meadow.

'Peak House', was an elevated, Grade 11 listed manor house, set in sixty acres of parkland, with eight cottages and a stud farm. Painted in soft pink, the front edifice was imposing. Jenny's hesitancy about the whole weekend almost persuaded her to turn around and drive home when it came into view. Her little Peugeot circled a water fountain by the front door. Before she got out, she took a deep breath.

A set of oak double doors faced her, one was half open. What does a girl do in this situation, she thought. Ring the bell and wait for a butler, or simply lug her suitcase out of the boot and trundle it up the six wide tapered steps. Her dilemma was answered when Anthony Rathenberg came out to meet her. A red setter bounded out from behind him.

'Jenny, how wonderful. Thanks for being early. I'll have time to show you around,' Rathenberg said. 'And you've brought good weather. Marvellous.'

The dog sniffed around the hem of her skirt.

'Come away Cotswold,' Rathenberg shouted.

The bespoke suit he wore at the office, had given way to a check shirt and cravat, shoulder padded pullover, corduroy trousers and brown brogues. He whisked her case out of the boot, and guided her, on his arm, up the steps, into an oak panelled hall of baronial proportions.

'Mary will show you to your room,' he said, handing her case to a woman in her late thirties, dressed in black and white maid's attire. 'I'll wait down here while you get organised,' he said, as he let go of her arm. 'Would you like tea, or a drink before the guided tour?'

'Some fizzy water please. It was a warm drive.'

She followed Mary up a curved staircase, wide enough to take a car, to a large second floor bedroom with a four-poster bed. The window commanded a view of an oval lake, half covered with water lilies. Peering out she could see the westerly aspect of the parkland; a stallion pranced in the nearest paddock. Mary returned with her fizzy water on a silver tray.

Trying to compose herself into some kind of sensibility she took time unpacking her case. This house, this lifestyle, was a mile away from anything she had ever known. She knew, therefore, she had to tread carefully.

Anthony Rathenberg was waiting in the hallway when she returned downstairs.

'Do you feel up to looking around?' he asked.

'I'd love to,' she replied, glad of the excuse to be occupied.

Keeping up a lively dialogue of history and anecdotes, he escorted her through three floors, four reception rooms, an orangery, an indoor heated swimming pool, a period barn and most of the stud farm. To Jenny, it was eye-opening, awe-inspiring and a little bit overwhelming. By the time she returned to her room, an hour later, she was exhausted.

Deciding her attire for the evening had been simplified by only bringing three suitable outfits. A white blouse and black skirt was that evening's choice. Most of the family were gathered in an oblong, high ceilinged drawing room, for drinks, when she ventured downstairs. A Steinway was raised on a dais at the far end. The furniture was large, chunky, and mostly oak. Tall arched windows opened up a vista of manicured lawns and flower beds, profuse with salvias, like a crimson carpet.

Besides the family members she already knew, Anthony's sister, Cordelia, a partner in a London firm of Estate Agents, had appeared. In turn, Rathenberg introduced her to Bill and Penny Bowles, two of Gerald's horse racing chums and Tyrone Oliver, famed London Welsh historical biographer, who knew also Casper. Jenny dearly wished she had Helen Dumas' taste in clothes, as she stood amongst them, sipping martini. The other women wore dresses of classical style, the men, lounge suits and ties.

'This pretty little diamond is on the trail of that bounder Casper Watkins,' Gerald Rathenberg said when he sidled over, while she was talking to Oliver. Broad, and way over six foot, Oliver's rounded, weather beaten face bore the tan of a yachtsman; 'his real love', he'd been telling Jenny. Bushy white hair swept back off his forehead, added to the ebullient illusion.

'For her sake I hope she doesn't find him,' Oliver retorted. He was drinking gin and puffing on a large cigar. 'No woman's safe with that man.'

They laughed and Jenny could feel herself blush.

'Now my dear, tell me what you've been able to find out,' Rathenberg said. He tilted his head closer to hers and searched her face.

'Not very much I'm afraid. Finding his Agent murdered in his apartment rather took the wind out of my sails.'

'Oh dear. Yes of course, that must have been awful.'

Fortunately for Jenny the dinner gong sounded.

'We'll have a little chat later,' Gerald said and moved off to organise his guests.

The dining room was spacious. Gilded in gold, three sets of ornamental chandeliers dangled precariously over the long narrow table. The glasses and cutlery below glittered in their reflected glow. Dark mahogany was the predominant style of the furniture. Being seated next to Tyrone Oliver was demanding. His hands tended to wander as much as his conversation.

'Editing fiction must be a bleak experience nowadays,' he ventured during the beef consommé.

'Oh I wouldn't say that,' Jenny replied, trying to remain diplomatic. 'It has its moments like any other job.'

'Much of the fiction I read is so dispiriting; everybody's either a manic depressive on drugs, or going through a messy divorce, with a handicapped child. It's all so predictable.' Oliver argued.

'You obviously don't read the right books. I've got a new author, Susan Barton, who writes wonderful, uplifting stories. It's going to be out in a couple of months, why don't you buy it and see.'

He turned his head to look at her fully.

'They're obviously very lucky to have someone like you at Knott and Pearson,' he said, while squeezing her knee.

Every time she glanced at Anthony Rathenberg he smiled at her. Cordelia kept looking across at the two of them.

'Wouldn't it be easier if you two sat together,' she said eventually, when he made a big fuss of serving Jenny with potatoes. Tall, like her brother, with blonde hair, frizzed into a mass of curls, she was strongly articulate and talked in a rapid-fire manner, as though she was addressing an auction. Unused to being the centre of attention Jenny was embarrassed and struggled to digest her coq au vin.

'They tell me you're from Wales?' Oliver said.

'That's right. The North, a little place near Mold.'

'Excellent,' he exclaimed, his eyes lit up. 'I'm from Bala, just down the road. We'll have to get to know each other much better.' He squeezed her leg again. She grabbed hold of his hand somewhere in the middle of her thigh.

After dinner they all settled in the lounge and Oliver entertained them with some readings. Like a chapel preacher, indulging himself with his Sunday flock, his deep Welsh voice resonated to pieces by John Betjeman, Dylan Thomas and Tennessee Williams.

'We'll have a bit of a party tomorrow night,' Anthony Rathenberg said at the bottom of the curved staircase, when they were turning in for the night. 'How about taking the horses for a gallop before breakfast?' he asked.

Jenny hesitated. 'As long as you find me one that's quiet. It's a long time since I've ridden.'

'Leave it to me,' he said. She took the image of his smile with her to bed and dreamt about it all night.

At seven thirty next morning, in the stable yard, the air was chill, the breeze fresh and the idea of riding wasn't nearly so appealing. 'Blackie' looked anything but quiet. Fourteen and a half hands of potential trouble was Jenny's initial reaction. She didn't possess a pair of jodhpurs. Dressing earlier, she guessed her Levis would cause her endless agony later. Cordelia, whose presence seemed to annoy her brother, had lent her a wind-cheater.

'I've never known you up so early,' Rathenberg said to her, while they mounted.

'Somebody's got to chaperone this young girl and I need the exercise,' Cordelia curtly replied.

A swirling sea mist drifted in off the channel as they clattered out of the yard. Fumbling with reins and stirrups Jenny found the experience daunting. Six years had elapsed since she last got on a horse. Out on the road they broke into a trot. Quickly it became evident that Jenny's rise and fall was completely out of cinque with the horse's stride patterns.

On the downs, a canter was frightening, breaking into a gallop, terrifying. Blackie was completely unresponsive to any of her commands. She clung on to his mane, the reins, the saddle, anything she could grab hold of. The animal's sole ambition was to catch up with his mates. How Jenny stayed on she didn't know. Grip with your knees, she remembered her riding instructor saying. Sliding around on the saddle in a pair of denims made that impossible.

'This is the life, eh Jenny,' Anthony Rathenberg said at the turn. 'You ride well.'

Before she could reply, Blackie was away again, flying with the breeze. By then, every muscle, every sinew, every bone, in her body was screaming with agony. When it was over and she was back in the warmth of the house, the muscle aching numbness outlasted her bath.

'How did you get on with Blackie?' Anthony Rathenberg asked at breakfast.

A right little bastard Jenny wanted to reply, but diplomacy won again. 'Very invigorating,' she said.

'Glad you enjoyed it anyway,' Rathenberg said. 'Tyrone and father are playing golf this morning, with Bill and Penny. I thought I'd walk the wood with Cotswold if you feel up to it.'

Cordelia had mentioned at the stables earlier that she and her mother were going into Brighton. 'A grand tour of the clothes shops,' she'd mentioned. 'You're welcome to come.'

The offer was tempting. However, their price range Jenny thought, would be just a little over her means, so she settled for the walk, hoping it might loosen some of the stiffness.

At the north west corner of the meadow-land, a deciduous forest of oak, ash and elm, encircled by Scots pine, had been planted by Tony's great grandfather in the nineteenth century. Originally, the plan had been to screen off the village from the big house, but the enterprise had progressed since then.

'We've lost a lot of trees, elm to disease and the gale of eighty seven,' Rathenberg explained as they set off. Cotswold followed, pursuing his own itinerary in the undergrowth, then periodically rejoining them on the path.

'This Casper Watkins business has resulted in one benefit anyway,' Rathenberg said as they walked. She was already having trouble keeping up. His long legs took one stride to her two and her calf muscles still hadn't calmed down from the ride. 'What's that?' she asked breathlessly.

'Meeting you. I'm afraid I hadn't noticed you in the office before. I mean I think you're such a stunner. I do hope you're enjoying the weekend.'

'Tony, you're going to have to slow down. You're walking too fast. I can't keep up.'

'Oh, I am sorry. There, is that better?' he said altering his pace.

'Yes, thank you.' She was flustered enough, without having to run. ' You're words are very flattering and I am enjoying myself, but I'm in enough hot water already over all this.'

'Oh,' he said and stopped. 'But we're only just getting to know each other. I know I can be a bit pushy, but give me time please.'

Jenny looked at him. A meandering, shallow stream gurgled alongside the path beside them. Cotswold made one of his periodic returns and jumped at her, leaving muddy paw marks on her jeans.

'Cotswold, get down,' Rathenberg shouted.

'I mean the Casper Watkins business, not you,' Jenny said, attempting to rectify her verbal error, while brushing at the mud. 'Henson's murder did upset me. Imogen's right really. I should stick to doing my job.'

'Yes, yes. It's inconsiderate of me to pressurize you when you've been through so much trauma.'

A sympathetic smile crossed his face. The breeze fluttered a wisp of his fair hair and his blue eyes warmed like the ocean when the sun settles on it.

'Let me show you the copse,' he said when they began walking again. 'My father planted it when my grandfather died, as a testimonial to his work.'

He guided her over a little bridge that crossed the stream, to a path alongside a heavy duty wire fence. Eventually they reached a gate with a padlock, which he unlocked. He called out to Cotswold who caught up. Inside the fence, massed ranks of azaleas, rhododendrons and bamboos, fought for space with specimen trees; Monkey puzzles, Acers, Cherries and many more, all in about an acre and a half of land. The foliaged enclave surrounded a small lake, with a timber summerhouse, built on stilts, on an island in the middle.

'I love coming here,' he said. 'It's so peaceful.' A small rowing boat tied up on the bank was needed to reach the summerhouse. Rathenberg helped Jenny on board. Close and touching like that her heart skipped numerous beats. Cotswold had to remain on the shore and whined when they rowed off. Rathenberg guided the little craft to the summerhouse, using a small paddle. Getting ashore involved another arm holding procedure. They were close enough to kiss, but Jenny jumped quickly for the bank.

The building was constructed entirely of timber. The door was secured by two padlocked iron bars. Surprisingly, the air inside was warm. Jenny looked around. Photographs of the estate, dating back to the last century, hung on the walls. Rathenberg knew the history of each one and described every picture knowingly. Four generations of his family were recorded in that summerhouse, all of them pictured with their estate workers, at locations around the manor house. He knew all their names, what they did, how long they'd worked there, when, and sometimes, how they'd died. Jenny observed his enthusiasm.

At the side of the timber house was a tiny balcony, jutting out over the water. For a time, while the sun edged through the trees, they sat together closely on a wooden bench, watching the trout leap, as he related the family forays in publishing. Jenny watched his face. Regularly it became animated, while he recounted some specific event. It was a face she could quite easily fall in love with, she thought.

They spent most of the day alone together. For lunch, they dined on crab salad in the dining room of the big house. Later, in the Rolls, they toured the local beauty spots. All the time he talked with authority on everything. As the day unfolded her perceptions of him changed, from employer, to one of a suitor. She found it flattering and stimulating, but also a little bit daunting.

Until that evening she hadn't given Anthony Rathenberg any encouragement whatsoever. She hadn't flirted, acted coquettishly, or even fluttered an eyelash when she gazed into his blue eyes. Up until then, she had just enjoyed his company. Her reactions had been purely platonic; more curious than anything else. However, a little bit of devilment had always featured in her character. A yen to explore; to take one step further than normal, just for the hell of it, sometimes intervened, not always to her advantage. Often that extra step had got her into trouble. It had taken her to Turkey. It had brought about the few sexual relationships she'd known. It had caused her to pry into Casper Watkins' life.

Wallowing in her bath before dinner, contemplating the evening ahead, a tinge of that devilment surfaced. These people are inherently wealthier than I'm ever likely to be, she conjectured. Listening to Anthony Rathenberg's chronicle of his family's history had been enlightening. Their progression in publishing often seemed to occur as the result of some illicit sexual liaison. Inter-marriages between various branches of the publishing industry seemed the norm. Her conclusion was that something more than just hard work was required to climb the greasy pole in her chosen career.

So, after her bath, she added just a tad more perfume than usual to her body, fussed at her hair with the curling tongs a little longer and chose the skimpy black cocktail dress she'd brought, together with strappy black sandals that had the highest heels she possessed.

Downstairs, in the drawing room, everybody was gathering for dinner. A villager, hired for the evening, was playing melodically on the Steinway. The room sparkled, the faces glowed, the conversation was raucous, the champagne pink. Dinner jackets and black tie, silk and jewels, plunging cleavages and exposed backs were evident. The golf had been a cliff-hanger, the shopping expensive; Anthony Rathenberg beamed at Jenny when she entered the room.

'You look absolutely marvellous,' he said. 'I've arranged for us to sit together,' he continued in a half whisper. He made it sound like a secret rendezvous, known only to them. This time, when returning his smile, she did flutter her eyelashes. And when she pretended to look into the glass of champagne he handed her, she did lean forward, just a little.

At dinner Anthony Rathenberg sat on one side of her and his father on the other. Like a spectator at a tennis match, she had to twist her head from side to side to listen to their anecdotes. They alternated with salacious tales about the early days of publishing. Each man determined not to be outdone by the other. Angling her head attentively, gazing into their clear blue eyes, their excited faces became a mirror image. Constantly they plied her with wine. By the end of the main course, the machinations regarding the route to the top in their world became more lucid. A healthy sexual appetite was obviously a pre-requisite. Jenny was having the most enormous fun.

After dinner, a bass player and a drummer teamed up with the pianist, to provide music for dancing. During brandy's each guest was invited to perform a party piece, something she'd been forewarned of. Fortunately, during her bath she'd given the matter some thought. When her turn came she was nervous. She stood up hesitatingly.

'As there are two of us here from the Principality, I've decided to sing something in Welsh,' she said. The room went quiet. 'I'm only going to do this on the condition that Tyrone helps me with the chorus.' She looked across at him. The others heckled him into submission.

'I'm going to sing Calon Llan, a Welsh hymn.........'

Tyrone got up, stood alongside her, and put his hand on her shoulder. Her voice croaked during the first verse, but when he joined her in the chorus, the nerves were gone and she crescendoed to a big finish. She sat down, relieved and embarrassed, to wild applause.

After that Anthony Rathenberg commandeered most of her dances. Limbs, still sore from the early morning ride nagged like a toothache, but every time she tried to sit one out he was back pleading for more. By eleven o'clock she just had to cool off. The veranda doors were open and she wandered outside.

Stars twinkled overhead in the clear sky. A dew covered the surrounding grass. It wasn't long before Anthony Rathenberg was standing behind her, with yet another Marguerite in his hand. The moon was casting shadows of the big oak trees across the meadow. She kept her back to him and felt him move closer.

'Jenny it's been wonderful having you here this weekend. You've made it such a treat for me.'

She turned to face him, returned his smile, and for a moment they held each others gaze, then he handed her the Marguerite.

'I've enjoyed it very much. Everybody's been so kind.'

'Do you think we could possibly see each other, up in town, in the week?'

Everything in her head went in a spin. Suddenly the notions of fantasy she had conjured up in her pre-dinner bath were now dangling in front of her with unnerving clarity. The opportunity to cash in on a large slice of one-upmanship, the chance to be indulged by a wealthy, handsome suitor, the olive branch away from penury, were at that moment reaching out to her with the hand that Anthony Rathenberg was placing on her shoulder.

'I'd heard there already was a lady friend,' she said, desperately trying to keep the quake out of her voice. His eyes searched hers.

'Marcia you mean?' His hand remained on her shoulder. Her skin tingled. She nodded.

'That's a long standing thing that's never really got anywhere,' he said. 'There was an idea we might marry. I did propose once. She told me it would interfere with her career.'

'Tony I am sorry.' She took a large gulp of the Marguerite.

He was still standing very close. Her instinct was to fall into his arms. Allow herself to be wrapped up in the warmth and security of his masculinity, the three generations of wealth, almost certainly the high profile career at Knott and Pearson. In fact, everything she'd ever desired.

'Tony I don't know what to say. You'll have to give me time to take it all in. I mean I had no idea you felt like this. All this is such an eye opener,' she said and waved her arm at the house and the meadow beyond. 'I'm only a country girl from North Wales.'

For a moment he looked stunned. 'Of course,' he said eventually, 'I hadn't thought of it that way.' The smile returned to his face. He removed his hand from her shoulder. 'You don't realise things like that when you're smitten.'

'Please don't misunderstand me. I am extremely flattered. There's nothing I could think of that would be nicer than seeing you. It's just a bit of a shock, that's all.'

'Yes, yes. Perhaps I could ask you again next week, on neutral ground so to speak.'

'Oh yes please. I'd like that very much.'

'Good. Come on then, we'd better rejoin the others or they'll think we've run off already.'

He took her arm and guided her inside. For the rest of the evening they danced or sat together.

It was well after midnight when the party folded. In her room her head was spinning. She couldn't decide if it was it from the wine, the brandy, the Marguerite's or Anthony Rathenberg's attentions. Sitting by the open window, taking in deep breaths, while running her fingers sensuously along the carved wood of the expensive dressing table top, she was desperately attempting to put her feelings into context. At half past one she gave up and sank into the deep down of the four poster. But sleep wouldn't come for a long time.

Next morning she decided to miss out on the early ride. She got up leisurely, tidied her room, then strolled the grounds, savouring the ambiance, while totting up the pros and cons of a relationship with Anthony Rathenberg. A post alcohol headache made her grateful for the brisk breeze that fluttered the oaks. On her way back to the house she met Cordelia, who was returning from the stables.

'You should have come. It was lovely this morning,' she said bustling up. Devoid of her expensive clothes and high heels, she could have been a girl from the village.

'My limbs haven't recovered from yesterday,' Jenny replied.

'And I expect you have a lot to think about,' Cordelia said.

'H'm,' Jenny replied.

'We're a demanding family. All pretty competitive I suppose. But from what I've seen you'd cope and be well liked.'

When they reached the house, Cordelia dashed off to the kitchen, while Jenny made for her room.

Sunday lunch was a beef roast. Everybody was present. Memories were exchanged, experiences shared. Afterwards she and Rathenberg walked the grounds with Cotswold. Then she made her excuses to leave.

'There's some work I have to finish off,' she said. 'If it's not done by the morning, I'll have Imogen on my tail.

'Oh dear,' he replied. 'We'll speak in the week then?'

'Yes Tony, we'll do that.'

Driving her Peugeot back to London, the weekend seemed like a dream. The house, the grounds, the family, the guests, the riding, the dancing with Anthony Rathenberg, his handsome face. Never in her life had she known such a time.

CHAPTER

DESPITE IMOGEN QUAITH'S CONTINUED ALOOFNESS, JENNY WAS glad to be in work on Monday morning. After another sleepless night something other than notions of romance were needed in her head. Notwithstanding the insomnia, a conclusion still hadn't been reached about Anthony Rathenberg; a decision, she guessed, most girls would find simple. Work therefore, was the only antidote for the malaise.

That Monday, simmering manuscripts, soon to boil into real books, were reaching deadlines. Frank Swan was continuing to issue more circulars about disappointing sales figures. 'Let's hope the next book will turn the corner for us,' he wrote. Pointed memos from Anthony Rathenberg reiterated the importance of 'making every decision cost effective'.

Sometime in the middle of that morning, at the height of all the frenzy, the telephone rang on Jenny's desk.

'Jenny, it's Casper.'

With everything else that had happened he'd temporarily slipped from her mind. Having turned him down last week she really didn't expect to hear from him again. In many ways she hoped she wouldn't.

'Oh hullo. Where are you?' she replied.

'I'm in town. Can I see you please, it's about the book. I need your advice. Could I take you out for dinner tonight? You said you would.'

Unlike before, his voice now contained the enthusiasm of one of her new authors, and at that moment Frank Swan's recent memo was staring up at her on the desk.

'I didn't say I would, I said I'd consider it, but if you think it will be helpful to the firm in producing another best seller, then I'll be happy to see you.'

With her every word, a four alarm bell rang in her head. She still hadn't mentioned to anyone about meeting him.

'Great,' he said, 'there's a heavenly little fish restaurant I know in Chelsea. If you tell me where you live I'll pick you up.'

She wasn't agreeing to that. Outside Acton Station would suit her fine. Give her time to change and compose herself. A silly thought ran through her head. 'I wonder if he's taken Caroline there?'

'I'll be in a red Ferrari. You can't miss it,' he said.

Over the previous few days Casper had been busy organising the requirements of living at his mother's cottage. He'd found a good Tesco near Mold and arranged for the Ferrari to be parked behind the old garage in the village. The business had been closed for five years. Mister Hartley, the owner, was retired, but he remembered John and let him park it round the back, out of sight.

'Wouldn't have minded servicing that,' he had said, admiring the car's sleek lines.'How's your mother, boy?'

To the local people of the village, money and wealth belonged in the outside world. It was something that was never likely to come their way, so they didn't bother acquiring the accompanying airs and graces that went with it. After discussing his mother's health, old Hartley wanted to know about London and where Casper lived; what was the size of his apartment and 'how much does a meal cost in the West End then?'

'Never!!' he replied when told. It took Casper an hour to get away, but for the first time in years he enjoyed talking to someone, just for the sake of it.

Twice a day he visited the hospital. The staff were aware of his fame, but conversations centred on the practicalities of growths and lymph nodes, radium and sickness. They were doing what they could. Each time he visited, his mother managed a weak smile.

In the evenings, mooching around the cottage, boredom set in. Poking in the awkward corners of the living room he re-discovered the contents of his father's bookshelves. He remembered his dad constructing them out of odds bits of timber he'd reclaimed from a building site. 'They'll hide the undulations in the walls and where the furniture doesn't fit,' Casper recalled him saying.

Alan Watkins aspired to write. He would scribble short stories and write simple poems. Mostly they were about the village and the people around. Having received no formal education, composing anything publishable was out of the question. His pride however, was in watching his son realise those dreams.

Reaching into the dusty shelves behind the settee Casper found a veritable library of classics. Amongst them, covered in plaster dust, was an English translation of the 'Four branches of the Mabinogion'. The yellowing pages, stuck with damp, contained a selection of tales about an heroic age before the coming of the English into Wales. Dating from the eleventh century, stories of romance and drama, based on the sagas of Celtic Gods and Goddesses and the life and death of their hero, Pryderi, were told. Casper became fascinated. He read them, over and over. Delving further amongst the cobwebs he found the stories of Arthur and his knights and the 'Treason of the Long Knives', when the Britons were forced to cede large areas of land to the Anglo Saxon invaders.

These stories stirred his literary juices and gradually unhinged his creative imagination. When he'd lived at the cottage in West Wales he'd wanted to write about something similar, but somehow the ideas wouldn't form. The outcome of his conversations with Ivan had put him on a similar tack. Now, from his father's simple, home made bookshelves, in the confines of his childhood home, he'd found the catalyst he sought.

In the long hours between hospital visits, he began. With biro and loose sheets of paper, he scrawled pages and pages of almost illegible script. His heroine was Catrin, a young girl, who like generations of daughters before, had been promised to an older prince. But this girl had spirit. As a child, she'd fallen for a beau from a far off land. In Casper's story, she eventually connives and murders her way into his arms. The more Casper scribbled, the more he realised the girl he was writing about was the girl from Knott and Pearson. The blonde haired nymph, who had emerged from the shores of his West Wales bay. Jenny Millington had unwittingly become his muse. She was his Catrin of Preseli. 'Of angelic face and sylph like figure, her slender fingers flew over the strings of the harp,' he wrote in his story.

At that point his text was a jumbled mess of contorted sentences. But at least it was a start. A story to arouse his imagination, a tale to be told.

To set it out properly he needed his word processor. That was back in London. To fire his descriptive prose, he also needed to see Jenny Millington. He needed to watch the way her mouth curled when she laughed; the way she sat up; the way she sat down; the steps she took, the sighs she made. He needed to feel the texture of her hair in his hand. The way her blue eyes drew him in; feel her breath on his skin. Really, he needed to be her lover.

CHAPTER

JENNY THOUGHT CASPER'S FERRARI WAS SOMETHING ELSE. JUST looking at it's sleek red structure when it drew up outside Acton station, was enough to set her hormones tingling. Fortunately the red of her new dress, a lunchtime purchase from Dickens and Jones, didn't clash. A tight fitting little number, with thin straps, revealing lots of flesh, produced a suitable reaction when she slid into the passenger seat .

'Gosh you look great. Thanks for coming. I like the dress. Hope you'll like the restaurant,' he ventured as she fastened her seat belt. A surge of motorised power catapulted them away. As he drove they talked about North Wales.

'Do you miss it?' he asked.

'I miss the people and the countryside and I don't see my family enough, but all the action's here, isn't it?'

'Yes, you're quite right. I can see you're not just a pretty face,' he said. She looked across at him. He was smiling. She hadn't seen him like that before.

'Scallops,' was a basement diner, with subdued lighting and fishnet draped walls. Hooks, rowlocks and oars, strategically aligned in amongst the netting, attempted to create a Mediterranean illusion. The waiters wore hooped blue and white T-shirts and matelot trousers. The menu looked complicated. Casper guided her to spider crab and sea snails, fried in deep batter, followed by a concoction of John Dory, halibut, hake and prawns. She happily listened as he described how it would all be cooked.

'How is your mother?' she asked, after the waiter had taken their order.

'Oh, not very good,' Casper sighed, 'I still feel at bit of a heel really. I should have kept more in touch. I've got to thank you though for letting me know. It was very brave of you.' He lifted his glass in a toast and clinked it against hers. They were drinking chilled white Rioja. Looking into his face was like trying to complete the clues in a crossword. A beard, now almost a full set, made him look more earthy, more sanguine, than the bland publicity photographs she'd viewed on his file. And he'd cleaned up well. A blue shirt and cravat with a corduroy jacket, over designer jeans, was a big improvement on his West Wales cottage attire. But most of all, being close to him in those surroundings, she could feel the pent up passion. Outwardly he didn't display it, but she could sense it, somewhere in his demeanour, bursting to get out.

'And Trevor?' she asked. He stared at her. They had been provided with wooden cutlery and he scooped a mouthful of snails from the dish, with the fork, before replying.

'Oh, you've found about him as well, have you? You have been a busy girl.'

'I walked right into it I'm afraid. Quite innocently. I was trying to find you and he was there when I called at the cottage.'

'And what do you know about him?'

'Not a lot. Only that he referred to your mother, as mother.'

'H'm. He had to go back into care. I've made some enquiries about a residential home. There's one nearby that may take them both. The doctors tell me my mother won't be able to go home, not initially anyway, so it's a way they could be together.'

'I am sure she'd like that.' The crab melted in Jenny's mouth as she talked.

'And I've decided to base myself at the cottage for a time,' he said. ' I can write there, and be on hand to see them most days.'

They looked at each other. There was a warmth in his face, but something else as well, something different. In a way it was scary. She couldn't put a tab on it. The matelot returned to take away their first course plates.

'And the book?' Jenny asked, when he had gone.

'Well as I said on the phone, I need your advice on that. It's different from anything I've done before. I'm not really sure about it.

You haven't mentioned anything at the office yet, have you?' His eyes were questioning, fiery.

Their main course arrived. Mounds of John Dory topped her plate.

'Oh gosh, good job I didn't have any lunch,' she said. 'No, I haven't said anything yet, but somebody's bound to find out you're around sooner or later. They've got a firm of detectives looking for you.'

'I know, I know. That's why I'm going to stay at the cottage. Get my head down. You know I find I can write better there. It's strange really. Going back after all these years has been quite therapeutic.'

'I'm very pleased to hear it, but what do you need my advice on?'

He stopped eating, put down his knife and fork.

'I'd like you to read what I've written Jenny. See what you think. There's about thirty pages so far. It's untidy and it'll need tightening up but it's pretty feisty.'

She looked up at him, he'd begun eating again, shovelling fish into his mouth like a little boy at a bun fight. But then her mind recalled the vitriol he used about alterations to his text. She didn't want to be subject to that.

'I couldn't improve on anything you could write,' she said.

'But this isn't like the other books. It's a different genre. You'll understand when you read it.'

'Well what's it about?'

'I'd prefer you to read it first. I'd like to know, off the top your head, what you think. You're reading books all the time. You'll know if it works. If Henson was around I'd ask him, but we both know that's not possible.'

Across the table their eyes held again, just for a few unaccountable moments. Enough though to send a charge of electricity bolting through her system. Enough to make the backs of her knees grip the seat of her chair and to store up a hornets nest of turmoil in her heart. Serious disorder was breaking out in her emotions. He spoke again.

'I've managed to put the first thirty pages on the word processor. Before I show it to the firm, I'd genuinely like your honest opinion. It would mean so much to me. If you don't like it, or you don't think it works, please tell me, it'll save a lot of time. If it's no good I'll settle down and write a sequel to 'Flame in the Sky'.

She stared at him, not really knowing what to say, afraid to comment, unsure of the right response. She hardly knew this man and there'd been so much gossip. Why was she trusting him like this. Her job was in jeopardy. She was out on a limb. Yet somehow, already, they almost felt intimate.

'Come on Jenny. What do you say? I won't bite, honestly. If dear old Henson was here he'd tell you that.'

Their eyes met again. The mention of Henson's name stirred memories. 'Casper's basically a good man,' Henson had said when they met. 'Unfortunately, there are times when he gets led astray by people who are attracted by his aura,' he'd added.

She put down her knife and fork. The meal was becoming a struggle.

'But if I don't like it, you'll get cross.'

'No I won't. At this stage, I don't even know if I like it myself.'

Suddenly her appetite was gone. She gulped at some wine.

'Casper I don't know. I only deal with new authors.'

'Well here's our chance to have a go at the big time together. If it's any good, I'll insist on only you dealing with it. Look, it's only ten minutes back to my apartment. You can read it there.'

'Casper I just couldn't do that. There's too many bad memories. How could I concentrate on anything after what I saw there. I don't think that's a good idea at all.'

He looked crestfallen. The waiter appeared again.

'Have you both finished?' he said.

'Go away!' Casper shouted. 'We'll call you when we want you.' He turned his head back to Jenny. 'What about your place then?'

'I'm not Caroline Di Angello,' Jenny said forcefully.

He rocked his head back and laughed.

'Thank heaven for that. You don't think I'd trust her with anything as important as this, do you. Have you met her?'

'Yes, in the process of my enquiries.'

'You are very thorough aren't you. What did you make of her?'

'Not a lot. Very glamorous though.'

'Oh she's that all right. About her only redeeming feature I'd say.' His face was beaming.

Jenny sniggered.

'Look Jenny, I'd be grateful if you could read it, that's all. I've got a copy in the car.'

Their eyes held again.

'If you take me home now, I'll read it tonight,' she said.

Outside her flat, he reached over to the back seat of the Ferrari and handed her a sheaf of foolscap paper, bound by an elastic band.

'That's my number,' he said, writing it on the first page. 'I've enjoyed this evening Jenny and I really would like your opinion on this.' He held up the manuscript with his right hand and placed his left one on her arm. As she was about to get out he spoke again.

'I could sit out here and wait while you read it. This is London Jenny, it's not late for London.'

She took the manuscript from him, then shook her head.

When she reached the foyer she heard the Ferrari roar away. Ignoring the lift, she removed her shoes and ran all the way up the five flights to her flat.

The red dress slid sensuously off her shoulders when she unhooked the straps. Looking in the mirror, for the first time in years, she felt nubile, desirable. She allowed her hands to wander down her bosom. As they slid, she could feel that element of devilment rising again. All this time with no man to speak of and now there were two, she thought. Both wealthy, both sophisticated and both interested. She smoothed out the dress, put it on a hanger in the cupboard and settled on the divan in her bra and pants, with Casper's manuscript.

The opening lines took her by surprise. It was completely unlike anything he'd written before. The first paragraph led straight into the plot and within what only seemed like a few minutes she'd finished the thirty eight pages. She was stunned. In that time she hadn't moved, hadn't even fidgeted. She'd been going to make a night-cap, but the cup was still by the kettle, waiting to be filled. This is dynamite, she thought, putting the papers down. For a long time she sat on the divan, re-reading passages here and there, letting the descriptions bask in her brain.

Her bedside clock said eleven. She made the drink, changed into her night things and returned to the divan to read it all through again. When she'd finished her opinion hadn't changed. What she'd read was absorbing and riveting.

It was nearing midnight when she put out her light, but her mind wouldn't settle. Through her window the streetlights of Acton twinkled back at her, while his tale of Celtic tribes revolved around and around in her head. Before sleep came, the phone rang.

'What did you think?' his voice said at the other end.

She shot upright. 'How did you get my number?'

'When you write thrillers you learn these things. I haven't disturbed you have I?'

'Yes, you have disturbed me. I was trying to get to sleep, but it's very difficult with all that murder, rape and sodomy still in my head. Did all those things really occur?'

"fraid so. According to the history books anyway.'

'I thought it was going to be about changing Britain into a Republic?'

'Same story, different century,' he said. His voice sounded soft, romantic. She curled her legs up underneath her and rested the phone on the pillow.

'Is this girl Catrin going to be the central character?' she asked .

'Yes, but I need to do some more research. I'll have to go to Aberystwyth. The NationalLibrary of Wales there will have more detail. But what did you really think? Is it any good?'

'Casper it's brilliant. I shan't sleep, I'm too excited.'

'It's only a beginning Jenny. Only ideas at the moment. I need more substance, more facts, more time. That's really why I phoned you. Before you say anything to the firm, I'd like to complete a hundred pages. Then that'll really give them something to chew over. Could you perhaps not say anything about me 'til then. Please, it's important I get it right.'

A whole host of thoughts flashed through her head. Everything she touched seemed to revolve in a circle. Casper, Anthony Rathenberg, Henson, her career, her love life, they were all whirling around and she was in the middle. He cut in again.

'Just for a while Jenny. I've only just got going on this. In a few weeks we'll have something to show the world. Please.'

What could she lose she thought. Nobody knew she'd seen him. And, if this story turned out to be a success, it could save them all.

'Oh all right,' she said. 'But it had better be worth it.'

'It will be worth it Jenny, I promise. If you're in North Wales at the weekends you could help with the editing. I can do so much more if somebody edits it as I go along. Henson used to do that. Would you help? I can get on with it better in North Wales. What do you say?'

She hesitated, curled her legs up even more.

'I'll think about it. Now I must go to sleep. I'm very tired and I've got work in the morning. Thank you for the meal and the story.'

'Good night Jenny,' he said and rang off.

Sleep came very quickly then. There were no dreams she could remember, just deep, suspended consciousness.

CHAPTER

Finalisation of the McHugh novel forced Imogen into breaking her silence with Jenny. The whole package was required at the printers by the end of the week.

'I've settled on these,' Imogen said, laying out prints of the art work she'd chosen on Jenny's desk.

'Fine, if that's what you're happy with,' Jenny replied, without looking at Imogen or the prints.

'Well what do you think?' Imogen said and lit the cigarette that was plugged expectantly in the end of the holder.

'I haven't had an opportunity to look at them. If you and Angela have chosen them I'm sure they'll be fine,' Jenny retorted, with her head still down on the papers in front of her.

'Bloody hell, why have you people have got to be so difficult? When I ask for your opinion, all I get is a load of waffle.'

For the first time Jenny looked up at her. Fire filled Imogen's eyes, fires of jealousy, Jenny guessed.

'If you'll give me ten minutes to look at them properly, I'll be happy to give my opinion.'

'For God's sake!!' Imogen said and stalked off, leaving the prints on Jenny's desk. 'The messenger's got to deliver it all to the printers after lunch,' she shouted back from her office doorway, then slammed the door closed. When Jenny looked around all the others in the room were grinning at her. She shook her head and they all laughed.

Later that morning the internal phone on her desk rang.

'Jenny, it's Tony. How are you?' Her body went rigid.

'I'm fine,' she said, trying to keep her voice down and also trying desperately to avoid saying his name. 'I haven't had a chance to thank you for the weekend,' she continued quickly. 'It was wonderful. I did enjoy it so much. It's just we've been so busy finalising the Mchugh novel.'

'That's good. What do you think? Have we got a winner?'

She wanted to say it wasn't a patch on the story she'd read last night.

'If we can get the release date right, I think it's got every chance.'

'Good, good. Look Jenny I've got to go away on business for a few days, but could we have dinner later in the week. I should be back Thursday night. Could we meet up then?'

'That would be very nice,' she said, almost in a whisper.

'Wonderful. I'll ring you at home on Wednesday night then. I'll know more of my schedule by then.'

She hesitated for a second. Imogen's door opened and she heard her call across the room to somebody else.

'That'll be fine,' Jenny said, lowering her voice even more.

'Excellent, excellent. I look forward to us getting together then,' Anthony Rathenberg said with enthusiasm and rang off.

When she looked up everybody in the room appeared to be staring at her. She grabbed the art work off her desk and held them up in front of her face, pretending to study them.

That evening, when she arrived home, a large foolscap envelope lay amongst her post. In the envelope was a bundle of A4 papers, tied together by a piece of string. Tucked into the string was a photograph of Casper dressed in a dinner suit and black tie, holding onto a bronze figurine.

On the first sheet of paper Casper had written, 'The unpublished words of the man from nowhere,' with a note underneath. 'Enclosed is the next forty pages. Would you please edit it, together with what you already have. I'm going to Aberystwyth, but should be at Mold by the weekend. Why don't you come up and we could go through it together. Also, there is a photo of the figurine, in case you remember seeing it at my apartment. Please excuse the dinner jacket.'

In the picture he looked different from the way she had come to know him. In his best bib and tucker he appeared sophisticated, debonair, almost conceited. She much preferred him as she knew him now. But she'd definitely never seen that figurine before. On the bottom of the page he'd scribbled the telephone number of 'Cartref'.

CHAPTER

THE FLUTTERY BELL PINGED. KATHERINE WALKER LOOKED UP AND her eyes did a double take.

'John, where the hell have you been?' she said. It was three weeks since she'd seen him. Under the counter his mail was mounting up. She'd been getting worried and even asked the postman to call at the cottage. 'The place looks closed up,' he'd reported.

Somehow he looked different. Better groomed, yes, but more than that. The hung dog facial expression he sometimes bore was missing. The eyes looked brighter, the reflexes more active. She noticed he'd grown the beard, but he'd also lost that desolate, scruffy look. His clothes were smarter, his hair was better kept; she wondered.

'Had a few family problems Kath. Things to sort out,' he said, almost cheerfully.

'You might have let me know.'

'Sorry, it was all a bit of an emergency. I had to make a dash.'

'To North Wales?'

'Yes, as a matter of fact. How did you know that?'

'A little bird told me.'

They stood looking at each other in awkward silence.

'Has there been much mail Kath?' he said, eventually.

'There's quite a pile for you here John,' she replied and delved under the counter.

'I've arranged for it to be redirected from now on, ' he said.

She was gathering the envelopes into small bundles and looping elastic bands round each one. She stopped momentarily on hearing his words. 'It's not been a problem John,' she said. There was more silence before he spoke again.

'My mother's not very well Kath and I am going to have to spend some time near her for a while.'

'Oh I am sorry to hear that. You've never mentioned anything about her before. I hope it's not serious?'

'Well she's very old and when they get to that age, if they're ill, you never know.'

'I am sure she'll be pleased to have you around. I do wish you'd said something about it before though.' She was still holding on to all his mail.

He nodded his head and reached out for the letters, but she didn't pass the bundles over. Their eyes held again for a second; hers pleaded, his eventually looked away.

'There's so much I don't know about you,' she said. 'Somebody else mentioned you were a writer. You never told me that either.'

'I didn't think it was important. I haven't done much for a few years now anyway.'

She looked at him again, searching for some flicker of acknowledgement, some hint of contrition, but he kept his eyes down.

'Will you be coming back to the cottage?' she said stuffing the letters into his grasp. Some of them spilt on the floor.

'I hope so Kath. It all depends on my mother I suppose.' He bent and scooped the mail into his arms, then turned and headed for the door. 'I'll pop in when I return,' he said without looking back.

She watched him pull the door open. The bell pinged and he walked outside without another word.

When he'd arrived, she'd been busy cleaning out the deep freezer and hadn't noticed the Ferrari. Through the shop door, for the first time, she could see its gaudy redness. He threw the mail in the back and bent into the drivers seat. There was a throb of twin exhausts before the car turned and pulled away.

A box of frozen peas was resting on the counter. When he came in, she'd been stacking them into the deep freeze. She picked up one of the packets and hurled it at the door.

'Bastard,' she yelled as the packet flew through the air. It split on impact. The contents spewed on the floor.

The cottage felt cold and damp. It took him an hour or so to clear up his belongings. On his way out he stood in the doorway and reflected. The place had served its purpose, he surmised. Without his meagre possessions it looked desolate.

He'd paid the agent the rent until the end of the month and told him he didn't expect to be back. Then he drove up the west coast road to Aberystwyth and the National Library of Wales.

There, for three days, he read, wrote notes and photocopied from nine in the morning until they closed at six. Their archives held all the background material he needed.

A small two star hotel on the front provided adequate accommodation. Each night, after dinner, he'd walk the promenade, then go back to his room, to type up his notes, until his eyes became impossibly blurred by the incandescent light of the word processor. Not a drop of alcohol touched his lips in all the time he was there, but by the end of the third day he was exhausted. That night he crashed out, half clothed, on top of his bed and slept 'til morning, dreaming of his Catrin of Preseli, or was it Jenny Millington, he wondered next day.

From Aberystwyth he journeyed to 'Cartref' via Machynlleth and the Cambrian mountains. The roads were quiet, the scenery breathtaking; maybe he would retire there, when the book was finished, he thought.

CHAPTER

JENNY MILLINGTON WAS IN A QUANDARY. SHE DIDN'T KNOW HOW long she could continue without telling somebody about Casper. In work, she and Imogen were constantly involved in a set to. She was also on tenterhooks about Anthony Rathenberg. If she accepted his offer of romance, the repercussions around the office were too awful to contemplate. Throughout the day her nerves were on edge, half expecting either of them to telephone when Imogen was around.

In the evenings, at home, she proof read Casper's story. His tale about Welsh princes, fighting over women and land, gripped her imagination. Assiduously, she made notes about each page, on a separate sheet of paper, then typed them out on her lap-top, before printing out a final copy of her thoughts. It was usually well into the midnight hours before she tumbled into bed, exhausted.

To keep things moving in the day, lunch was usually taken on the run; a sandwich and a plastic mug of tea at her desk, while working. Unfortunately the habit became counter productive. Imogen had also developed the same lunchtime routine and often they'd end up having a row.

One day, to get a break from it all, after finishing her sandwich, she decided to go for a walk. It wasn't far to the old shops of Hammersmith. The sun was up and for a few brief moments it was good just to stroll in the warmth, stretch her legs and mingle with the populace.

Nothing more than window shopping was possible. Her finances were too low for anything else. As she strolled her mind was ruminating over where the plot might lead in Caspers' story, when suddenly, something in the window of a second-hand shop made her stop and stare.

For a moment she thought tiredness was playing tricks with her mind. One of her night time dreams spilling into the day, she presumed. So she took a deep breath and moved closer to the shop window. Now she could see it clearly. It was much bigger than she had imagined. About two foot in height, it had an ugly sphinx like head that glared back at her. But from what she could remember, it was the bronze figurine in Casper's photograph. She rubbed her eyes and looked hard again.

Inside, the shop was a scruffy mess of a place, selling anything. Arty paintings, pictures, statues, vases, china pots, ornaments and crockery. Gingerly she looked around. It was all very untidy. Pots were stacked one on top of the other, pictures lent up against tables and chairs, a thick layer of dust covered the surfaces. The window area was open to walk into and she took a few tentative steps towards the figurine.

'Can I help?' A tall, dark skinned, heavy man, probably Pakistani, said and wandered over. She pointed to the figurine.

'Could I have a look?' she asked. He puffed when he reached into the window. Three gold rings on each hand shimmered in the reflected light from outside. His waistline bulged when he bent, causing a blue speckled shirt to splay out of the back of his trousers. He handed over the figurine without comment.

It was heavy. A smooth lacquered finish made it slippery to hold. The base was circular. Jenny turned it over, then round and round in her hands, inspecting it closely . There was no inscription.

'Where did this come from?' she asked.

The man shrugged his shoulders and looked at her with little enthusiasm.

'House clearance probably,' he said.

'How much?' she asked.

He shrugged his shoulders again. 'Twenty five quid,' he said, with a disinterested face.

'Fifteen,' Jenny said. The man shook his head.

He paused, opened up his palms and said. ' Twenty.'

'Seventeen fifty,' she replied.

He nodded. There were no more words. She fumbled in her purse and handed him two ten pound notes. Most of the change was given in five and ten pence pieces, individually fished from the depths of his trouser pocket, until at last he produced a pound coin to complete the transaction.

Wrapped in her jacket, she smuggled it into the office, and hid it in her desk drawer for the remainder of the afternoon. The same camouflage was used at home time.

That evening in her flat, perched on her only table, in dwindling light, its lustrous bronze glow glared at her, like a genie's lamp. All through her meal it stared, making her nervous, giving her indigestion. After washing up she searched for Casper's note and telephoned 'Cartref'.

'Casper, I've finished the editing,' she said, when he answered.

'Well done. What do you think?' he replied. It was over a week since they had spoken. The warmth in his voice gladdened her heart and dispelled some of her doubts.

'It's very good. No, it's brilliant. Just what we need at the office. When can I hand it in?'

'You can't do that,' he bellowed harshly, then quickly added. 'Not yet anyway. Jenny I've got so much material from Aberystwyth and I'm only just beginning to work that into the story. I need a bit more time. Let's get at least a hundred and fifty pages done while it's going well.' His tone had mellowed. She could sense the excitement in his voice.

'I thought you said a hundred pages.'

'I know, but that was before I knew about all this background material. Don't spoil it now. This could be really good.'

She knew it was good. The pages she'd seen told her that.

'How's your mother, before I forget to ask?' she said.

'Oh about the same. No, some improvement I suppose. She's eating a bit now.'

'I'm pleased about that. Casper, there's something else as well.'
'What's that?'

'Well I need to see you to explain. When are you coming down?'

'Not for a bit. I want to crack on, while the iron's hot.'

She hesitated. She wanted to tell him about the figurine, but then she didn't want to break his concentration on the writing.

'I may come up and stay with my parents at the weekend,' she said. 'Would you have any objection to that. I could show you my notes on the editing at the same time, if you want.'

'You're not going to be one of those over zealous, fussy editors are you? I couldn't stand that.'

'No, you're the writer. My comments are on a separate sheet. You can throw them in the bin if you like.'

There was a pause.

'Look, why don't you come over late Saturday afternoon,' he said. 'We can go through what you've done and then I could take you out to dinner. Anyway I've missed your pretty face. I seem to write better when you're around. What's this other thing?'

'I'll tell you when I see you.'

When she put the phone, down she sat for a long time in the dark, staring out of the window, not really looking at anything, just letting her mind run over his words. His voice excited her. Its tone, its tempo, seemed to caress her ears.

The telephone ringing brought her back to reality. She half thought it might be Casper, about something he'd forgotten. She nearly said his name when she answered.

'Jenny, I'm glad I've caught you in.' It was Anthony Rathenberg. She swallowed hard.

'Tony what a pleasant surprise.'

'Jenny, this business matter I'm involved in is taking longer than I expected,' he said. He sounded breathless. 'I can't see me getting back 'til Friday. I was hoping we could meet up before then, but it doesn't look as though it's going work out.'

'Don't worry Tony, perhaps we can get together next week,' she said.

'What about the weekend?' Rathenberg said. 'I could stay in town if you're around.'

Jenny hesitated.

'I promised my parents I would visit them this weekend.'

'Oh well, perhaps next week then,' Rathenberg said.

They talked some more about the Mchugh novel and the Barton book and then he rang off. Straightaway she rang her mother.

'You sound upbeat my dear. A new boyfriend perhaps?' her mother said, after discussing the arrangements. How was it mothers always knew, Jenny thought.

'No mother, it's nothing like that. I've just got an interesting bit of work on at the moment. That's why I'm coming up. The author I was telling you about before is staying at Gwernaffield, and I've been helping with his text. So we are going to meet up over the weekend.'

'Oh how exciting,' her mother said.

CHAPTER

KNOCKING ON THE FRONT DOOR OF 'CARTREF', CLUTCHING TIGHTLY onto a plastic bag containing the figurine and his manuscript, she was wondering what to expect.

'You timed that well,' he said when he pulled open the door. His smile was welcoming. He looked smart in a blue and white chequered shirt and fawn slacks. The beard had been trimmed. 'I've just about finished writing. My you look very sexy,' he added.

What to wear had been a problem she'd mulled over since breakfast. A white fluffy mohair pullover and tight black slacks won the day in the end.

'I didn't want to get here too early in case I disturbed you,' she said as she walked in. The cottage looked different, new table lamps had been acquired, vases of cut flowers adorned the cupboard tops, the fire was glowing in the hearth. He lent forward and kissed her on the cheek. She could detect cologne.

'Your unpublished words,' she said, pulling the manuscript from the bag and handing it over.

'Oh,' he replied.

'And my notes,' she added, delving further into the bag.

'Oh,' he repeated.

'The story's good enough without my intervention, but they may help.'

'I shall read them with interest,' he said.

'And there's this,' she said, pulling out the figurine. It nearly slipped through her hands.

For a moment he just stared. His features froze. She held it out in front of him and watched his expression change.

'My God, where did you get that?' He grasped hold of it like a cherished possession.

'Is it yours? The one in the photograph?'

He inspected its head. Ran his hand over the top. Turned it upside down and looked underneath the plinth.

'Yes. Oh yes, it is. How on earth did you get hold of this? That's wonderful.'

Suddenly he pulled her into his arms and hugged her, pressing her body into his. She felt the figurine dig into her back. He kissed her on the mouth; the intensity shocked her. She stood back and the look of joy on his face was for real. He pulled her back again into his arms. This time she responded. They kissed, this time more passionately, more desperately. Inside his mouth, her tongue began a journey. A journey of discovery, searching for his essence, deep into the depths of his soul. It was a long time before they parted.

'Where in the world did you find this?' he said breathlessly.

'I sort of stumbled into it,' she said as he guided her to a chair by the fire.

'Well, this calls for a celebration,' he said, after she'd explained. He disappeared into the kitchen and returned with two wine glasses and a bottle of champagne. He filled the two glasses, then sat opposite and watched in silence, studying her, as she sipped the champagne and told him about her haggling with the shopkeeper. The bubbles tickled her nose and made her giggle, but when she looked at him, he seemed enchanted, spellbound. She felt flattered, but slightly embarrassed.

Later, over chateaubriand at the Hanbury Arms, they dissected the bones of his tale of 'Catrin of Preseli'. Their eyes flashed fireballs at each other across the table.

'You're very good at your job,' he said at one point, after reading some of her notes. 'I wish I'd known you a few years ago. I'd have probably written more books.'

She smiled and flicked her hand at her hair.

'Jenny, I want you to help me with this novel. Will you do that?' He reached out across the table for her hand. Slowly he moved it to his lips and she felt the warm texture of his beard brush across her fingers, as she nodded her acquiescence.

In the cottage, she sat at his feet, by the fire, supping brandy, while he read to her the new pages he'd written. Occasionally she'd raise a point, or make a comment and he would stop and jot a pencil note in the margin. While he read, he stroked the nape of her neck. Sitting there, with her back pushed into his knees, the vibes between them intensified. Gradually, the gentleness of his hands on her neck and shoulders stirred her emotions and she began losing control.

Upstairs in the tiny bedroom, with its sloping ceiling, control was totally lost. Only tangible sensations and blissful feelings existed and she floated like a queen in the soft succulent down of his embrace. Up and down, like a roller coaster at a fairground, she travelled, touching heights of ecstasy she'd never experienced before.

Afterwards, she lay draped across his body and wondered how it had suddenly become this crazy. Was it all a moment of madness, an accumulation of happenings or just the release of tension after all the trauma and pressure. At that moment she didn't know and couldn't care less.

It was the early hours of Sunday morning before she crept up the stairway of her parents home. She'd removed her shoes and from memory she thought she knew where each individual creek in the treads were located. Annoyingly however, her feet discovered some new ones in the woodwork since she'd left home.

'You were working late last night,' her father said at breakfast next morning. Jenny kept her eyes down on her bowl of cornflakes. 'Does this man pay you overtime?' he added. Fortunately it was just the two of them in the kitchen; mother was still in bed. Their eyes met briefly.

'We didn't finish working 'til late. Then he took me for a meal and afterwards I had to put what we'd done on the computer. Life's tough in publishing,' she replied.

Her father snorted, puffed a cloud of pipe smoke into the air and carried on reading his newspaper. She got up and cleared away the dishes.

'I told your mother you'd probably met up with some of your old pals at the pub,' he said when she removed his plate. Their eyes met again. On her way to the sink, with their plates, she placed her hand on his shoulder.

Later, with her father, she walked the golf links behind the house, a regular jaunt when she was a child. In May they'd harvest elderflowers, from which he'd make champagne. In August sloes, for sloe gin and in September mushrooms. Each time they'd go home joyous, with carrier bags laden, full of their pickings.

'You never ever heard from Terry again?' her father asked during their walk.

Terry Williams had been her only real love. Tall, with pale blonde hair, a local farmer's boy, they were childhood sweethearts, went to the same secondary school. He was her first lover. Once she went to University, however, things changed. On one of her weekend breaks at home, he announced he was joining the Merchant Navy. 'We'll write and I'll see you when I'm on leave,' he'd said. He never did write. The last she had heard, he was sharing a flat with some of his pals in Southampton. It broke her heart.

'No dad,' she replied to her father's question. 'He obviously preferred the sea.'

Spending most of the day with her parents had reinstated a degree of normality in her mind. In the homely atmosphere of 'Plas' the wild uninhibited emotions of the previous night, with its heightened bodily desire, were given a chance to cool down.Her mother cooked a traditional Sunday lunch, and while they dined she brought Jenny up to date with news of Isabel, Duncan and the kids. The two hours when they were together was like a flash back in time. A period of simple pleasures and family life; time to discuss ordinary mundane matters. It didn't last long. After lunch, she made her excuses to leave. 'I need to get back to London early,' she said. 'I've got to put yesterday's work on a disc before Monday.'

She wondered what her parents thought about her current lifestyle. Throughout the weekend they'd mostly listened and made polite responses to her tales of work and London life. But throughout, their expressions had been fraught with doubt. As she drove away that afternoon and watched them disappear in her rear view mirror, she wondered how her life had become so severed from those secure roots.

But of course she didn't drive straight to London. She drove first to Gwernaffield. On Saturday night Casper had said there were more pages to edit. When she arrived at the cottage, they were arranged in a tidy pile on the table.

He helped remove her coat, then, before she had time to say anything, he pulled her into his arms. Urgently, their lips re-united and the passion of the previous night returned. When they parted for air she struggled free.

'Are these the pages you want me to check?' she said moving towards the table.

'I've done quite a bit this morning as well,' Casper said. He was standing behind her. While she looked at the first few pages he began to stroke the nape of her neck. 'You must be very good for me,' he added. 'I don't know when I've written so much, in such a short time.'

The touch of his fingers on her body made her spine tingle. The stroking motion of his hands soon developed, deliciously, into a massaging rhythm, causing her concentration to waver.

'Let's leave this for a while,' he said pulling her up into his arms. 'There's more interesting things we can do upstairs.' Willingly she succumbed.

Like the tide breaking on the shore, the waves of passion engulfed them both as they rolled around together on the squeaky mattress. Afterwards, while she dressed, he lay on top of the sheets, watching her.

'I think I'll stay on here for a few days and get on with this chapter while it's hot,' he said. 'But I should be in London by Tuesday. Perhaps you could show me the second-hand shop where you found the figurine?'

'Don't you think you should leave that to the Police,' she replied while buttoning her blouse.

'There's more to it than just the figurine,' he said, then briefly told her about the missing half a million pounds.

'Casper that's awful.'

'I know, but there's got to be a reason why he did it,' he continued. 'I've known the old bugger most of my life and I'm convinced he wouldn't defraud me. I must try and find a way of getting into his house. He used to keep all my accounting records. There may be a clue there about why he did it. Trouble is the police won't let me in'.

'Casper please be careful. Henson was brutally murdered. I saw that. Shouldn't you leave it to them.' She turned to the mirror and began combing her hair.

'You've met Palmer haven't you?' he said.

'Yes, unfortunately.'

'Well then.'

He got off the bed and slid his arms round her waist. She looked at the reflection of the two of them in the dressing table mirror. It was all like a dream. Casper Watkins standing naked behind her, with his arms wrapped around her shoulders. Then he started to nuzzle her neck and undo the blouse she'd just done up. Suddenly his hands, his lips were everywhere again. It was all too blissful to protest and they ended up back on the bed.

Midnight was approaching when she arrived back at Acton. Walking into her flat, hugging his manuscript to her chest, she was floating on air. The whole weekend had been surreal; she'd been living out her fantasies.

In work, on Monday, Imogen continued to be a complete bitch, but Jenny didn't care. All she could think about was Casper and the things they had done together at the cottage. Home time that evening couldn't come quick enough. The tangled web of intrigue he'd plotted in his story was bubbling into something dramatic and she was desperate to get on with the proof reading, to find out more.

During her lunch break another little corner of devilment entered her head. She went back to the to the second-hand shop. The same man was lingering in the shadowy corners at the back, when she walked through the door.

'I came in the other day and purchased a figurine,' she said. Once again he looked at her indifferently. 'It was a bronze thing. About two foot high. I saw it in your window. Do you remember?' She pointed to where it had been.

'Not exactly,' the man replied.

'I bought it for a friend,' Jenny said. 'He used to own one just like it. He said there used to be a pair. If possible I'd like to try and find the other one.'

The man continued looking at her blankly. He rubbed his hand across his eyes to illustrate his indifference.

'You couldn't possibly remember where you got it from, could you?' she said. 'My friend is poorly at the moment. If I could find the other one it would cheer him up.' She fished into her handbag for her purse and pulled out a ten pound note, which she held up in front of the man's face.

He stared at her, searched in his pocket for a packet of cigarettes and lit up before he spoke again. Jenny continued to hold out the note.

'Please,' she pleaded. 'My friend is not well.'

He drew hard on the cigarette. 'There's a man who brings stuff in from time to time,' he said. 'Big coloured man. The bar the gays all use, "The Dylan". I see him go in there sometimes, in the lunch hour. His name's Raul, I think.'

The cigarette smoke was getting on her throat.

'If he comes in again, could you ask him where he got it from. It would help me so much,' she said and lowered the note into his hand. 'I'll call in again at the end of the week.'

Outside on the pavement she gulped in fresh air and hurried back to the office.

At the end of the working day she was rushing across the road for the tube, when she heard a voice call out.

'I say Jenny, hang on. Wait a minute.'

The voice repeated her name. When she reached the other side of the road, she turned around and saw Anthony Rathenberg running to catch up.

'My, you are in a hurry,' he said when he reached her.

'Tony I am sorry. I didn't see you there. I was trying to make the five fifteen,' she chuckled, trying to cover her embarrassment with a smile.

'You're such a difficult girl to pin down,' he said. Dimples formed in his cheeks as he grinned. The sun was at an angle on his face, lighting up freckles she hadn't noticed before. 'I was wondering if we could have dinner this week?' he asked.

The wind was blowing her hair into her eyes. Surely this was all too good to be true, she thought. Two ardent suitors on successive days.

'That would be lovely,' she replied, trying to look coy. 'I've got something on tonight, but I'm free after that.'

'How about tomorrow?'

'Fine.'

'I'll pick you up at home?'

She nodded, looked pleased.

'About seven,' he said.

'If Imogen let us out by then.'

He laughed, looked boyish, 'Great,' he said and walked back across the road towards their office.

Sitting in the tube, watching the adverts flash by, she couldn't believe how her life had so dramatically changed in such a short time. Making love at the weekend with Casper was unlike anything she'd ever known. And now there was this other delicious man, who also wanted her. She was on a high, but, as the train sped on, the doubts began to deluge in like a tropical rain storm. What if? What if Anthony Rathenberg found out about Casper? What if Casper became jealous of Anthony Rathenberg? Worst still, what if Imogen found out about everything? Oh my God!! By the time she reached her apartment she was almost quivering with fright.

CHAPTER

THE MEMORY OF JENNY MILLINGTON'S NUBILE YOUNG BODY FUELLED Casper's literary juices. From the moment she had left him on Sunday evening, page after page of descriptive text had tumbled from brain to word processor, elevating his 'Catrin of Preseli' into the princess he desired her to be. But like an addict on a drug, he desperately needed more. Only the soft contours of Jenny's body, the delicate fragrance of her perfume, the sound of her gently pleading sighs, could unleash more of the words trapped in his brain.

Over the weekend he'd remembered where Henson used to keep a spare key to the patio door of his house. They'd used it one night returning from a drunken spree, when Henson had mislaid his key.

On Monday evening he visited his mother, then drove on down to London. It was two thirty in the morning when the Ferrari screeched up the ramp of a multi-storey car park, two blocks away from Henson's house. He walked the rest of the way through quiet, deserted streets.

A metal gate from the back alley led into the garden; they'd used that same entrance on the night he'd remembered. The gate was rusted with lack of use and overgrown with ivy, but he was able to shove it open, just enough to squeeze through. A sodium streetlamp on the pavement behind helped him to pick out the garden shed.

Fumbling about in the semi-darkness, cursing and swearing, tripping over rakes, forks and garden furniture, he eventually found the upturned flowerpot. Underneath, wrapped in a plastic bag, was the key. He'd remembered Henson saying the patio door had a special mortise lock, with bolts into the floor and he was hoping the police hadn't needed to secure it further. He reached into his pocket, put on a pair of gloves and headed for the house.

Magically, the key still fitted and the door opened. Stealthily, he crept into a downstairs lounge, then tip-toed towards the study. The room was a mess. Papers and books were strewn everywhere. He went over to the venetian blinds, angled them closed and switched on his torch. Most of the furniture had been stacked into the middle of the room. Around the untidy heap the corners of the carpet had been turned up. He guessed the police were looking for drugs. Henson used to keep his supplies in here.

His business account ledger and the statements were always kept in a drawer in the desk. To get at it he had to pull some of the furniture aside, but the drawer and the rest of the desk was empty, everything had been removed. Only a large blotting pad in a fancy leather holder was left on the top.

Casper recalled that one of Henson's fads was to insert a clean sheet of blotter into the pad every Monday morning. Usually, it was put on top of the previous sheet. He pointed his torch. On the top sheet, scrawled in Henson's scratchy hand, were lots of names and telephone numbers. Carefully, Casper wrote them all down in a notebook he'd brought with him. It took a long time. In all there were twelve sheets of blotter and diligently he worked through each one, writing down everything. On one sheet, 'Tuesday, draw out £100,000 in cash,' was written. In amongst the telephone numbers he spotted Caroline Di Angello's. When he'd finished, he carefully reinserted the sheets and put the blotter back on the desk.

He searched around for Henson's filofax, but it wasn't there. Behind the desk, on the wall, there was a calendar with pictures of Scottish mountain scenes. Casper noticed the letter 'R', pencilled in alongside certain dates and he added those to his notes.

Quietly he walked around the house, but it didn't feel the same anymore, so much had been disturbed, the sparkling charm of his old friend was absent. In those high ceilinged rooms they'd laughed until their sides ached and argued 'til dawn, cynically berating each other over some contentious issue. But always there'd been laughter. He was certainly going to miss the silly old sod.

At Ebury Terrace, in between bouts of writing, he worked through the telephone numbers in his notebook. Adopting a false name, he claimed to be a Solicitor, acting on behalf of Henson's estate.

'I'm trying to put together his last few days and your name was on his calling list,' he usually began.

News of Henson's death had obviously travelled the gay community. Some of the numbers were part of that fraternity and all he got from them was a few taciturn replies.

'B and R Enterprises,' a female Gaelic voice replied to one call. The name Ralph Brennan had been scribbled alongside the number. This time Casper tried a different approach.

'Can I speak to Mister Brennan,' he asked.

'Who's calling?'

'I'm a relative of Henson Littlewood. I was told to contact this number and ask for Mister Brennan.'

'Can you hold,' the female voice said.

'Hullo. Mister Brennan's not here just now,' a male Irish voice came on.

'Who am I speaking to?' Casper said.

'Fergus McCann. They're all over in Spain at the moment, filming. Is there a message?'

'Have you a number there I can ring?'

'Not really. They're moving about all the time, on location.'

'When will he get back?'

'He may be here for a short time next week,' the Irishman said.

'Perhaps you could mention I called. My brother has died and I know he was in touch with Mister Brennan about some business.'

'I will that,' McCann said. 'I'm afraid I didn't get your name?'

'Littlewood,' Casper said. 'I only have your number. Can you tell me where I'm ringing?'

'Dublin,' McCann said.

'And you're a film company?' Casper asked.

'That's right.'

Casper wrote the name and number on a separate sheet he'd been compiling of positive leads and drew a large circle around it.

CHAPTER

WRITING WAS AN EASIER EXERCISE WITH PRINTER AND WORD processor together at Ebury Terrace. By teatime on Tuesday Casper had completed another stack of pages for editing. Two days had passed since he'd last tasted Jenny Millington's delicious flesh. Therefore, he decided to take the completed pages over to Acton, take her out to dinner and see what transpired later.

He rang the doorbell. She was not long in answering. A look of horror covered her face, she was dressed to go out.

'Casper, you can't come here,' she berated, without inviting him in.

'I've managed to complete these,' he said holding up the pages of manuscript. 'Thought perhaps I could take you out to dinner.'

Instantly she was in panic mode. She moved out into the passageway, half pushing him away.

'You've got to go, now,' she said, making a shooing motion with her arms. 'Anthony Rathenberg's going to be here any minute. We're going to a publicity bash.' She grabbed the manuscript from his hands. 'Get away now, or he'll see you.'

He stood in silence, looked at her in astonishment.

'Go, quickly. Now, please, or it'll be curtains for both of us,' she berated.

In the melee, they both completely missed the figure emerging from the lift. When she heard footsteps in the passageway, she looked around and saw Anthony Rathenberg striding towards them, clutching a bunch of red roses. She and Casper froze motionless, like a wide-eyed pair of rabbits, caught in a car's headlights.

'Mister Casper Watkins, if I'm not mistaken,' Anthony Rathenberg said when he reached them.

Like a pair of burglars on a job, they'd been caught redhanded. The pages of manuscript in Jenny's hands weren't even in an envelope; bound together by an elastic band, the printed text was clearly visible. The two men glared at each other.

'Pardon me for interrupting,' Anthony Rathenberg said, as he looked at each of them in turn. 'You've been an elusive man to track down Mister Watkins. Obviously I should have looked closer to home.' Then his head moved to face Jenny. 'I'd like to see you in my office in the morning please Jenny.' Disdain filled his words and his expression. He turned and began to walk away.

'Don't be silly man,' Casper said, moving a few steps after him. 'I've been away on a sabbatical. I needed a break. This young lady helped me to get back. I've also started a new novel. It's going to be great.' He pointed at the manuscript in Jenny's hands.

Rathenberg stopped halfway along the passageway and turned to face them. The red roses were now in his right hand, facing downwards, already they seemed to have lost their allure.

'Well that's your business. Miss Millington seems to have forgotten who pays her salary. My office in the morning please Jenny,' he said, then marched off down the stairway, ignoring the lift.

'What's with the roses?' Casper asked.

Tears began to well up in Jenny's eyes. 'It's all such a mess,' she said. 'I don't know why I got involved in the first place. Whatever I try is always thrown back in my face.'

Casper guided her inside. When he'd shut the door, she fell into his arms and the tears flooded.

'I've said it all along Jenny, you're too clever for your own good. The rest of us try to do the best we can to make the wheels go round, but you're always determined to do things your way.' They were Imogen Quaith's words next morning, and they hurt the most. Jenny was sitting on the edge of a chair in Anthony Rathenberg's office and she had no real answer. Offering excuses about keeping quiet because of Casper's family problems fell on stony ground. Up until then Rathenberg had said very little. He sat behind his oval desk and just glared at her.

'Your contract requires you to act in the best interests of the firm at all times,' he then said. 'I suggest by concealing Casper Watkins' whereabouts, when you knew we were trying to trace him, was not that. And also, assisting an author who is under contract to us, without our authority, is another breach. I have no alternative but to suspend you, without pay, until the next partners meeting, when a decision on your future will be made.'

'But I have my mortgage to pay,' she cried out.

'I can't say any more Jenny. You are in breach of your contract. If you have any doubts, I suggest you read it or consult your solicitor. Now I must ask you to clear your desk of personal possessions and leave the building. I will be in touch by letter, after the partners meeting.'

The shaking in her body began in the tube, on the way home. Her head was still revolving with a host of unanswered questions. What would she tell her parents? How would she manage for money and why had she become so obsessed with this bloody man, Casper Watkins? Last evening, after he'd left, she wondered about his commitment to her. Was she just a plaything, while he was tied up with this book? When it was finished, would he discard her like all the others? His words of last night came back to her as the train hurtled along.

'If you were going to a publicity bash, why was he picking you up here, and why was he bringing you a bunch of roses?' he'd asked, inside her flat. By then she'd slumped tearfully in her only armchair.

'Oh Casper, I don't know. I expect he fancies me. I can't help that. You men are all the same. It's all such a mess,' she shrieked. Her tears continued to tumble again, red blotches covered her cheeks, she was dabbing at her face with a handkerchief.

'Well I have to get back to North Wales,' he said, almost coldly. 'My mother has more tests tomorrow and I promised I'd be there for the results.'

Her crying hadn't really stopped, the tears were still flowing, but he stood on the other side of the room appearing to be unconcerned.

'Perhaps you can ring me when you've had a chance to look at those,' he said pointing at the pages of manuscript. 'I'm going to drive up there now,' he added, and headed for the door.

Jenny didn't move. She was still in the chair, dabbing tears.

'I'm sure it will all work out,' he said as he left.

Sitting in the tube, going over and over it all, she nearly missed her stop. When she got home she tried to pull herself together. Absentmindedly she picked up the pages of manuscript he'd left last night and began to read. Concentrating on the plot seemed to relax her. It was about an hour before she finished. Straightaway she rang the Mold number, but there was no reply.

Her watch said just after eleven. She changed into a tight fitting roll neck top and jeans, went down to her car and drove into Hammersmith, looking for the 'Dylan'.

The traffic was busy, the sun was out. Her eyes, still sore from last night's crying, searched along the street as she drove. Not far from the second-hand shop, a painted hanging sign, depicting the Welsh writer in pose, smoking a cigarette, came into view. The frontage was mock Tudor. Hanging baskets, profuse with petunias made it look quite attractive. She parked opposite. By then it was coming up to midday and she sat in the car for some time, wondering if her courage would hold. But she'd come this far, she told herself. In for a penny in for a pound, she quoted, as she got out of the car.

'What'll it be sweetie?' The barman asked. Tall and thin, with a shaven head, there was a tattoo on each arm and a golden earring dangled from his left lobe. He wore a yellow and mauve striped vest.

'Oh, a glass of white wine,' she replied and glanced round while he fussed with the bottle. The bar was quiet. A handful of men, sitting in pairs, sat at tables in the corners.

'I'm looking for someone,' she said when he brought her drink. 'A guy who deals in bric a brac, antiques that sort of thing. Someone said he came in here. A big coloured man I'm told, named Raul, I think.'

The barman look at her questioningly.

'He's usually in most days, about one o'clock,' he said.

She sipped at her drink and moved to a seat away from the bar. More customers, all men, began to arrive. Each one who entered looked at her intently. She was still the only woman. Suddenly she felt hot, gulped at her wine and headed for the door.

A woman traffic warden was standing by her car.

'You've had half an hour love,' the woman said.

'I'm waiting for someone at that pub,' she answered, pointing in the direction of the 'Dylan'.

'Well, if you don't move now, it'll cost you a ticket,' the woman's cockney accent rasped. Mumbling to herself, she got into the driver's seat. Twisting her neck to reverse, she spotted a large coloured man walking along the pavement in the direction of the 'Dylan'. He was well over six foot six, with a shiny, shaven head. He looked like a West Indian fast bowler.

A car behind tooted his horn, wanting her space, but she just had enough time to see the coloured man walk into the 'Dylan'.

CHAPTER

'JENNY!!' HE EXCLAIMED LOUDLY.

She watched the expression on his face change from uncertainty to joy, as the cottage door scraped open. It was early evening, next day.

Her flat in Acton had become claustrophobic. A hundred times, or more, she'd gone over and over in her mind how she'd got herself into such a mess and it all pointed to Casper Watkins. Since his name first appeared on her lap-top, she had to admit that she'd been attracted to him like a moth to a flame. In Acton, she decided the only way to deal with it was to dive in and tackle the fire. For the time being her work was on hold, her life in limbo. At that moment this man represented the only positive, and so, after lunch, she drove to North Wales.

'This is a pleasant surprise,' he said, still holding onto the cottage door.

'I've finished your manuscript, and I've been fired.'

'What do you mean, fired?'

'Well, placed on unpaid suspension actually. For concealing your whereabouts, and reading your manuscript without their permission.'

'Can they do that?'

'They already have. Look Casper, are you going to invite me in, or do you want me to go.'

He stood aside. 'Oh and by the way, in case you're interested, I've seen the man who had your figurine.' When she brushed past him that same tingle she'd come to recognise flashed through her body.

In the tiny confines of the narrow lounge they stood awkwardly facing each other, not knowing what to say. His word processor and

152

printer were set up on the table; pages of printed text were littered around, a miserable fire spluttered smokily in the grate.

'Well I'm pleased to see you're working anyway,' she said. 'Almost makes my sacrifice seem worthwhile.' He was still standing, looking at her nonplussed. 'Considering everything, you could at least offer me a cup of tea,' she added.

A smile broke across his face and his eyes warmed. The same unkempt look she'd seen at the cottage in West Wales was back. His hair hadn't been washed and his clothes appeared slept in. He moved towards the kitchen without saying anything. She sat in the chair by the fire and wondered if this was the kind of reception she'd driven all this way for.

While they drank tea, she told him about the man called Raul. Gradually, as she related her escapade at the second-hand shop and the 'Dylan', he appeared to warm towards her. The odd word of interest or concern gradually began to seep out of his mouth. By the time her tale had been told he was sitting forward in his chair, with his hand on her knee, stroking it. Afterwards, upstairs, with rain clattering on the sloping roof, he made love to her and she felt secure again.

'So you mean this bastard Rathenberg has stopped paying you?' he asked afterwards. She was sitting cross legged at the bottom of the bed, munching on a piece of toast.

'Seems that way.' Her left palm was held upwards, underneath the toast, trying to catch the crumbs.

'Well he can go and fuck himself,' Casper said. 'He's not getting this story.'

'He says you're under contract to produce another book.'

'Bollocks. If it's as good as you say it is, I'll put it up for auction, sell it to the highest bidder.'

'Can you do that?'

'I'll bloody well try,' he said, propped up the pillows and sat up straight. 'This is where I miss old Henson. He'd know what to do.'

She brushed the crumbs off the sheet and slid on top of him.

Next morning, an aroma of coffee and toast tickled her nostrils. The bed alongside her was empty. A bumping sound from downstairs had woken her. For a moment, she couldn't think where she was. The low sloping ceiling, above her head, reminded her.

Casper was in the kitchen, making toast. The table in the lounge was laid. She'd never shared breakfast before with any man, other than her father. Casper was wearing an old blue pullover, with holes in the sleeves, jogger slacks and a pair of trainers. He grunted a greeting, but proper words were sparse. She helped carry some things to the lounge table, while he finished the preparations.

'What are your plans Jenny?' he asked tetchily. 'Do you want to stay here?' He began to spread butter on a piece of toast.

'No, I was just so terribly lonely in my flat after the other evening. I'll have to get back and try and sort out this business with Knott and Pearson. If I stayed here it would only worry my folks and I'd like to keep my work situation from them, at least until there's a final decision. Anyway, if I've got to get another job, it's going to be easier in London. What about you?'

'H'm,' he said crunching on the toast. 'I really need to go down the coast. There's a ruined church at St. Govan's and some places around St David's I need to check out. But in the night I thought a lot about us.'

She looked at his rugged face. There was no doubt she was in love with him. But nagging doubts still persisted about his commitment. She still half expected one day to wake up and realise it was all a dream.

'I have an idea,' he said gruffly. 'At the moment the historical stuff for this piece is only in rough notes.' He took another bite of toast and some marmalade ran down his chin. 'But I've written down, on my copy of the manuscript, where I want it all to be inserted in the story.' He slurped a mouthful of coffee. 'Look Jenny,' he pointed at her with the remaining portion of toast, 'it would save me a tremendous amount of time if you could work the notes into the spots required.'

'You mean help write the story?'

'Yes, if you like. It's only factual stuff anyway. You know what's required, I can see that, by the comments you've already made. I'll check it over afterwards, but it would help to keep things moving along. I'm willing to pay. Let's say two fifty a week, until it's done. That should help tide you over.' He said it all in a matter of fact way. Almost without enthusiasm, as though he was telling her what to get from the grocers.

She looked at him again. The whole idea of her joining Knott and Pearson was to be involved with writers; now, here was one of the best, asking her to help write a classic.

'Casper, are you sure?'

'Of course I'm sure. I'll stay on here for a couple of days more. I want to keep writing while it's still in my head and I need to sort out somewhere for my mother and Trevor. When that's done I'll go down to West Wales and then on to London. It'll be a few days before I get there,' he said, in a similar matter-of-fact tone.

She didn't know whether to hug or kiss him. She was about to drape her arm around his neck, but she noticed him flinch, so she withheld the impulse.

'Of course I'll do it, if that's what you want,' she said and reverted to her breakfast.

Driving south, later in the day, she felt surprisingly buoyant. Casper Watkins had induced feelings in her body she'd never experienced before, but those nagging doubts still persisted. Would the fire between them burn out when he had finished the book? Any moment she expected to come tumbling down off her magic carpet and wake up to the reality of a mortgage and no job.

Some of that reality faced her when she arrived back in her flat. A letter from Anthony Rathenberg, setting out the reasons for her suspension, was waiting amongst her mail. There would be a partner's meeting at the end of the month, he wrote, when her case would be discussed. Their decision would be final, but she had the right of appeal to an Industrial Tribunal. 'If you consider that, I suggest you consult a Solicitor,' he instructed.

Yet somehow, clutching Casper's bundle of manuscript, and having his word processor alongside her when she read the letter, softened the blow. His literary world of surrealistic Celtic Gods and Goddesses had corrupted her thinking and so far, deliriously blurred her vision.

'Is Seamus Brennan there today?' Casper asked. He was phoning Dublin from Gwernaffield, before setting off for West Wales. He'd spent the previous two days writing. The book was going well. Having someone else edit it, as he went along, meant he could crack on with the story. For the first time in years he really felt excited about something he'd written.

The doctors at the hospital said his mother was making progress. On one of his daily visits they indicated that they may be in a position to release her within a week so. During his time there, he'd also visited a nursing home and reserved two adjacent rooms for her and Trevor to move into, on her discharge.

'I'll see. Who's calling?' the female Gaelic voice responded to his call.

'John Littlewood,' Casper said. Then, one of those silly musical tunes came on the line.

'Seamus Brennan speaking,' a heavily accented Irish voice said, when the music stopped.

'Mister Brennan. I'm a relation of Henson Littlewood,' Casper said and paused, awaiting a response.

'Oh yes,' was the reply.

'Unfortunately he's been murdered.'

'I'm not sure to whom you are referring,' Brennan said, sounding impatient.

Casper decided to try something off the top of his head.

'Well there are some notes I found in his diary, about arranging money for a film project you are involved in. About half a million pounds it says. You are B and R enterprises?'

'We are indeed, but I know nothing about money of that sort. From whom did you say?'

'Henson Littlewood, he was a literary agent. The notes I have tell me that five separate amounts of one hundred thousand pounds have already been passed over.'

'And you say this man, your relation, sent it to us?'

'That's what his diary says.'

'Well I've no knowledge of that Mr Littlewood. There is a Venture Capital Fund that helps us with finance. Perhaps your relation invested in that. Money for that could have been transferred in stages.'

'Who would I contact about that?'

Brennan gave Casper the name and address of a London firm of Management Consultants. He recognised it as the same firm who handled Caroline Di Angello's affairs.

'Mister Brennan you've been most helpful,' Casper said. 'There is one last question. Were you ever approached about making a film of a book called 'Flame in the Sky'? It's by a Welsh author, Casper Watkins. He was one of my brother's clients.'

'I don't get involved with evaluations. There's another management team who do that. Filming is my bag. 'Flame in the Sky' you say? Could be, the title rings a bell. We've got so many projects on the go, titles don't mean a lot I'm afraid, unless we're actually working on them at the time. The management consultants will tell you though.'

CHAPTER

'RUM AND COKE PLEASE,' CASPER SAID. IT WAS LATER THAT WEEK AND he was in the 'Dylan'. The bartender was wearing a pink and green striped vest.

'Will you be wanting food?' he asked.

'No thanks,' Casper said and sat down at a table in the corner with his newspaper. It was ten to one, the bar was full. He recognised a few faces around him as literary people. Some of them glanced in his direction, but he averted his eyes and hoped the beard and the baseball cap would hold his disguise.

For nearly an hour he sat, slowly sipping his drink. He was about to leave when a large coloured man, wearing a white Panama hat, a beige lightweight suit and carrying a gold topped ebony cane walked in. He didn't quite fit Jenny's description, but Casper guessed this had to be him. The man joined a group at the bar, all men, some were coloured, some white. Casper guessed all of them were gay. He got up and went over to the bar.

'I'll have one for the road,' Casper said to striped vest. He was now alongside the big man, who towered over him.

'How's your love life Raul?' another man at the bar asked.

'Up and down as usual,' Raul replied. Those around him guffawed.

The bartender brought Casper's rum and coke and then served the big man. 'What'll it be Raul?'

'Pink gin,' he replied.

Casper watched his massive, soft hands pick up his drink. Hands like a baker, Casper thought, hands that would be good at kneading, moulding, strangling.

'You look like a man of business,' Casper said, turning to face Raul, after the big man had taken a sip of his drink. Huge, hazel, expressionless, doleful eyes looked at Casper over the top of his glass. 'I've got some antique trinkets I want to sell,' Casper added. 'Only a few bits. Not worth a fortune, but they've been taking up space since my parents died. Know of anybody locally who may be interested?'

The big man stared hard. Casper could feel his eyes drilling into him.

'What sort of things?' Raul asked.

'Oh, ornaments, nick-knacks, trinkets, bits of silver, that sort of thing.' He held his breath.

'I may be interested,' Raul said. 'Depends on the price though. If it's over a hundred notes, forget it.'

'Oh I'm sure there's nothing worth that much. Just family bits and pieces.' Casper said.

'Do you want me to have a look?' Raul asked.

'If you're sure it's your sort of thing. At the moment they're in a box in my garage. How can I get in touch?'

'I'm in here most days. If not Paul knows my number,' he said, nodding at the barman. 'Raul's my name.'

'I'm John,' Casper said. 'That's great. I'll be in touch then.'

Casper gulped down his drink and left quickly.

At Ebury Terrace, on his word processor, he'd made a complete schedule of all the names and numbers on Henson's blotter, listing them in chronological order. Four of them were repeated, and Caroline Di Angello also cropped up on several occasions, as did the number of the management company Brennan had given him. By then he'd obtained copies of his bank statements. They indicated that the withdrawal dates of the five, one hundred thousand pound amounts, matched the dates pencilled with 'R' on the calendar in Henson's study. Gradually he worked through the list when he wanted a break from his novel.

One day, he rose at dawn and worked through until evening, then rang Jenny Millington.

'How are you lover?' he asked.

'OK, I guess, where are you?'

'Ebury Terrace. I've been working since dawn. If I came over now could you make me something to eat.'

'What did your last slave die of ?'

'Love,' he said.

'Yes, I can make you something with eggs. How long will you be?'

In twenty minutes he was there. In another five, they were making love, struggling with the narrowness of her divan.

'You could come and stay at my apartment,' he said afterwards, while eating scrambled eggs. 'There's more room.'

'Too many horrors for me there. I've told you that before. Anyway I like my flat.'

He mopped some of the eggs off the plate with a piece of bread.

'I've seen your coloured man, Raul,' he said.

She stopped sipping at her coffee and looked at him.

'Where?'

'In the 'Dylan'. Big bloke isn't he?'

She looked at him wide-eyed.

'Casper! I really think you should involve the police.'

'What and spoil my fun. Have you ever heard of B & R Enterprises?' He was wiping the remainder of what was left of the eggs with the last piece of bread.

'No, should I?'

'Not necessarily. There's one of those bureaus in Acton High Street where you can do a company search. Would you do one for me, on them. There'll be a fee, I expect,' he said and fished a twenty pound note out of his pocket. 'If it's any more let me know.' He wrote the name of the company down for her, on a piece of paper. 'You might as well have this as well,' he added and from the same trouser pocket handed her a cheque. It was made out for a thousand pounds. She took it from him gingerly.

'Thought I'd pay you for the month, in case I have to give you notice,' he said.

When she saw the amount she clasped the cheque in both hands, close to her chest, as though it was the winning ticket for the lottery.

'I feel like a kept woman.'

'Good. All you have to remember then, is to say 'yes.' You can add 'please', occasionally if you like, but it's not important.'

'Who are B & R Enterprises?'

'A film company. Their name and number was written down numerous times on a blotter on Henson's desk.'

She stared at him.

'Casper!' she said.

CHAPTER

AMONGST THE MESSAGES ON CASPER'S ANSWER PHONE AT EBURY Terrace, he was surprised to have received one from Anthony Rathenberg.

'When I saw you the other evening, you mentioned that you'd started on a new book,' the publisher said. 'We were wondering how it was coming along? Now you're back in circulation, perhaps you could pop in for a chat. Please give me a call.' Cheeky bastard, Casper thought.

Minutes later the doorbell sounded. It was Jenny with his text and more notes. Her face had a sheen about it he hadn't noticed before; a white T-shirt and jeans showed off her figure. He pulled her into his arms and began smothering her face with kisses.

'No time for that now,' she said, holding his manuscript up above their heads. 'I've corrected this; it's full of spelling mistakes. Don't you use the spell check?' She was trying wrestle his hands away from her body while holding onto the manuscript. 'And I've worked in some of the bits you gave me. You'd better look at it before I do any more.'

He kissed her cheek, then both eyes. She struggled out of his grasp, but he pulled her back again. 'You're very good for me,' he said and then kissed her full on the lips.

This was her first visit to the apartment since that awful day when she found Henson murdered. The torture of her nightmares weren't completely exorcised, but if she was to climb her way out of the feeling of oncoming depression and cling onto her sanity, she knew she had to go back. Sitting together with Casper at his desk, that particular desk, was difficult. At least having him there and having his book to discuss, gave her something else to concentrate on. But it wasn't easy.

'I'll never feel comfortable in this apartment,' she said, while they were going through some of the text.

He put his arm across her shoulder and smiled at her.

'You are very brave Jenny. If this had been the other way round, I'm sure I'd have called it a day long before now.'

She looked at him. When they first met, at the cottage in West Wales, she couldn't ever imagine him saying anything like that. There was still a lot of him she didn't understand, but every day a little more was revealed, another chink became exposed and her fascination increased.

'I'm after your millions really,' she said jokingly. He laughed, then read through the pieces she'd written.

'This looks fine,' he said. 'Perhaps you should write all of it,' he added grinning. 'I'll give you the ideas and you can write it out. Save me an awful lot of effort.'

'H'm,' she smirked.

He put down the pages he'd been reading and looked at her.

'I've been thinking about a better way of doing this,' he said and sat back in his leather chair. 'When I was up in North Wales I put all the story on a master disc. But I'm so scared with all my travelling around of mislaying it, or having a computer blow up. Then I'd lose the lot. Perhaps you could hold on to the disc and we can update it when we're together.'

'I haven't got a machine anymore. I had to hand it in when I was suspended.'

He thought for a few moments.

'Well I'll buy you a new one then. We'll get a proper computer. Keep it at your place. Then I can download as I write, and you'll have the back up to edit. How about that for an idea?'

'Oh Casper,' she said and laughed. There was a sparkle in his eyes and a cheeky grin on his face. When he was like that she did so love him.

'Oh I nearly forgot,' she said. 'Talking about computers, I've got this search you wanted. You owe me a fiver by the way. It was twenty five quid.'

'Typical,' he said.

From amongst the clutter inside her holdall, she pulled out a handful of printed computer sheets. With the back of her hand, she pressed them out flat on the desk in front of him.

'They look like a lot of jumbled figures to me,' she said. 'But there's a few interesting things I noticed. It says here they're an Irish company, with a Dublin address. Seamus Brennan and Otto Rheinhart are the directors. There's also a German address. This is what caught my eye though.' She picked up the second sheet and placed it on top of the others. 'As you said, they're a film company. Do you remember the film 'The Two Alices'?'

'Sort of.' He pushed his chair closer; their arms and bodies were touching, it felt good. She continued.

'Well, it says here, they made that film. But here's the really interesting bit. What do you know about 'Listen to the Music'?'

'Absolutely nothing. But from the look on your face I can see I'm about to find out.'

'Look, here, it's mentioned in current projects.' With her index finger she pointed to a paragraph on the page in front of him. 'Casper, that's the film Caroline Di Angello is making in Italy with Claudio Karponti. I read about it in the newspaper. In the film Karponti's a deaf composer and she's his girlfriend. A few weeks ago I read filming had been held up due to a problem with funding.'

He looked at her. 'Are you thinking what I'm thinking?' he said.

'Yes,' she said.

'My money?'

She shrugged her shoulders, raised her eyebrows and looked at him questioningly.

That afternoon they went into Acton, bought a computer with a modem and a compatible lap-top. For the rest of that day, in her flat, they struggled to interpret the manual and apply the installation process.

'Thank God for that,' Casper said, when it eventually came on-line.

She laughed. 'Where am I going to eat my meals? This has taken up half my table.'

'You won't have time for that. I'll be in touch most of the day.'

'Huh!' she said. 'I know how to switch it off. At least I've understood that much of the manual.'

She looked at him. Again there was a smile on his face. He almost looked domesticated, something she thought impossible when they'd first met. The day had been fun. Tackling a complicated task, together, had been a pleasurable experience. Like the book and the sex, the things that bound them together were becoming a joint effort. She wondered if he felt the same. Unfortunately, he wasn't always expressive that way.

Afterwards, on her narrow, uncomfortable divan, they sat, side by side, sharing a tumbler of martini, just like a couple of teenagers, arranging their liaisons for the week ahead.

'I'm going to have to go up North tomorrow,' he said. 'The hospital wants to discharge my mother and I promised I'd be there to see her into the nursing home.'

'I'm so pleased. What about Trevor?'

'I'm hoping to get him in there as well. I can use the time in between to continue with the story. But when they're both settled, there's a few things down here I want to sort out, once and for all.' He emphasised the last four words.

She looked at him. The carefree, relaxed demeanour had gone. An expression of grim determination had taken its place.

A converted nineteenth century country mansion, in parkland, a few miles outside Mold was the nursing home Casper had chosen for his mother and Trevor. He'd arranged for her to have an en-suite, ground floor room, with a view of the gardens. The hospital organised an ambulance to take her there. On arrival the staff fussed over her. By the next day they'd organised a hairdresser and sorted out a chiropodist. Casper brought flowers, and some of her ornaments from the cottage. The warm smile he received when she was settled was his reward.

'You'll be wanting to get back to London, John,' she said on one of his visits.

'No hurry mother. I'm perfectly happy at the cottage, as long as Iris leaves me in peace,' he said, while holding her hand. 'And I've started on a new book. It's quiet there and I can get on with it. I'm not going anywhere until I've got Trevor settled in with you.'

'Oh John, you're always busy. Iris means well, you mustn't be rude to her.'

'Me rude. Mother, I've never been rude to Iris.'

She chuckled. Her throat rattled with the effort.

'I do miss my little home though. Do you think I'll ever be able to go back?'

'Of course mother. This'll only be a temporary thing. Until you finish your treatment.'

'I do hope so,' she said and looked at him wistfully. 'The garden will be getting in such a mess.' He squeezed her hand and they smiled at each other.

Arranging for Trevor to be with his mother wasn't so easy. All his records were registered in the name of Montgomery, his natural father. Also, his welfare was organised by the widows and orphans section of his father's regiment. Dealing with them and their bureaucracy, Casper regularly blew his top.

'I'm his half brother,' he shouted one day down the phone, to a woman administrator in Aldershot.

'But we've no record of your involvement before,' the woman replied curtly.

'I haven't been involved before, because I knew nothing about it.'

'Well we'll need to see documentary evidence of your relationship. And this nursing home you want to put him in, it might not be suitable for his long term care. He's a difficult case.'

'I know he's a difficult case. That's why I want him with his mother. She's in her eighties. I'm her son. I want them to be together, as they were at her cottage. You agreed to that, what's so different now?'

'It's not that simple. He's a ward of court. The trustees will need to visit the home,' the woman said.

'Surely this nursing home would be better than the cottage or where he is now? He'll be next door to his mother and there'll always be someone there to care for both of them.' Casper's temper was rising.

'It's a four star establishment. I can send you the brochure, and I'll be paying for it.'

'But I repeat, we have no record of you. His Trustees will have to meet you, and carry out a financial appraisal. He's got no money of his own. If at any time you couldn't support him, he'd have to go back into care. Shifting him about would be detrimental.'

And so it went on. Two or three weeks passed. Casper clung on desperately to his patience, knowing if he lost it completely he'd never get anywhere with these people. He was made to see a solicitor; swear affidavits; meet the Trustees. Two tall men, in dark suits, with even darker expressions. But they weren't completely convinced. A trial period of two months was agreed, with a review after that.

In between, he wrote, mostly at dawn, while his mind was fresh, before the problems of the day cluttered in. Later in the morning he'd go on the phone and argue with the bureaucrats. In the afternoons he'd visit his mother. In the evenings, organise his meal, phone Jenny and deal with her alterations to his text.

In the past his modus operandi was to dawdle away at a story until his publishers started nagging. But his new system of downloading and updating with Jenny worked well. By then he had three hundred and fifty pages completed. The occasional editorial disagreement did, however, surface.

'That's the third time you've altered the beginning of that chapter,' Jenny once e-mailed back in frustration. 'I wish you'd damn well make up your mind, I have to keep altering the history parts to fit in and you're eating up my copy paper.'

'But that chapter is now supposed to be a time shift.' Casper responded.

'Well please can you decide which way you want it, before you download it. If you had to traipse a mile each time for copy paper, you'd be more careful.' .

'But you're missing me though?' he e-mailed back.

She didn't respond.

Dealing with family problems was also a novelty for Casper. Throughout his life, until then, there'd only been his mother and father. His father died suddenly of a heart attack when Casper was in his twenties. And his mother, until her recent bout of incapacitation, had never suffered an illness in her life. In his work, anything of an administrative nature was dealt with by Henson. So being able to apply his best head of the family manner to his mother's and Trevor's affairs, greatly enhanced his self esteem.

He discovered that having a sibling on whom he could channel his pastoral energy, without fear of contradiction, to be an uplifting experience. He would breeze into the care home issuing demands and instructions to all those concerned. By then, they had learnt of his fame. 'Casper's, my brother. He's a f-famous writer,' Trevor had told everybody. So Casper's bombastic manner was just about tolerated, although behind his back the staff looked at each other with wary eyes.

Over the weeks visiting his half-brother changed, from being an annoying chore he could well do without, to something he almost looked forward to. His initial reticence over the man's shortcomings and disabilities disappeared when he discovered amongst those stumblings, dribblings and bumblings, the latent talent Trevor possessed in his sketching. So, on each visit, rather than take orange juice, or fruit, Casper would bring new HB pencils, erasers, paper, and pictorial books for him to copy from.

One day, on his arrival, Trevor was waiting for him in his room. As Casper approached he held out a complicated drawing.

'Another new sketch?' Casper queried. Every visit he'd been presented with a different piece of work. They'd all been scenes from around the home; the gardens, the rooms they occupied, or sometimes members of staff. This time however, Trevor had sketched a street scene, it was copied from a pictorial book Casper had brought in the previous day.

He took the crumpled sheet of paper in his hands and studied it. The detail of people and buildings was quite amazing. On the table, by Trevor's bedside, was the pictorial book, open at the relevant page. The texture of the clothes, the composition of the buildings, the camber on the road, he'd captured it all. Casper was astonished.

'This is really quite brilliant, old chap,' Casper said. 'Brilliant.'

Trevor gurgled, saliva appeared at the corner of his mouth. This agitation, Casper had come to recognise, was a sign that Trevor was getting excited about something.

'You're the wr-writer, I'm the ar-artist,' Trevor stuttered and a wide grin spread across his graceless mouth.

'That's right old son. Perhaps we should go into partnership?' Casper said, still studying the drawing. 'I'll write the stories and you can illustrate the chapter headings. How about that?'

Trevor gurgled some unintelligible response.

'I'm going to take this to some art friends in London,' Casper said, holding up the sketch.

Trevor gurgled to himself again and walked round and round the room, in circles, repeating his gurgling, just as he'd done the first time they'd met.

'Then, I'd be f- famous like you?'

'Maybe old son, maybe.'

After Casper had left and for the rest of that week Trevor told all his friends at the home that he was going to sketch the drawings for Casper's book.

Casper also told Jenny about it next time they spoke. 'This guy's sketching is something else,' he said to her on the phone. 'His talent's too good to ignore. When I'm up in town, I'll have to take his work to some of the art people.'

'You sound excited?'

'He's begun to fascinate me.'

The fascination resulted in Trevor's character being integrated into the story. 'I don't have to guess where he's come from,' Jenny wrote in an e-mail. 'Catrin' suddenly acquired a mentally retarded half-brother, 'Caradoc', who came to live with them from another family. In the story, from then on, through all 'Catrin's' trials and tribulations, 'Caradoc' was with her.

Jenny eventually complained. There were pages of alterations, mounds of backtracking.

'Yes, yes, I know, but does it fit in all right?' Casper queried.

'Of course it fits in. It's marvellous. When are you coming down? I miss you.'

'You could come up.'

'There's the partners meeting at Knott and Pearson next week. I don't want to come up before then. I'll have to tell my parents something when the decision's final, but I can't risk them seeing me in North Wales before that. But I do want to see you so badly.'

There was one very big reason why she wanted to see him. One morning, early, she'd had to leap out of bed and only just made it in time. Retching into the toilet, she guessed the worst. She'd been late before, but never that long. Sitting up in bed afterwards, sipping a glass of water, she wondered what to do.

A couple of days later a doctor confirmed her fears. 'Is the father aware?' he'd asked, diplomatically.

'No, he's away working just now.'

'Well you'll let me know if you have any problems,' he said with a sympathetic smile.

Problems, boy, have I got problems she thought. Considering everything, she was remarkably serene, almost smug. After all, she was carrying Casper Watkins' child. Perhaps half-expecting to be suicidal relieved the anguish, she surmised, laughingly.

CHAPTER

CASPER WAS CONVINCED THAT HENSON WOULDN'T HAVE DELIBERATELY defrauded him. He was, however, determined to get to the bottom of it, so he formulated a plan.

Tidying up his family affairs in North Wales took much longer than expected, but it did ensure that rapid progress was made on the book. The downloading and Jenny's editing saved months of time. It still required honing and polishing, but it was, at last, getting into a form to present to a publisher.

Watching Trevor sketching in his mother's room, at the nursing home one day, was enough to convince him that things there were reasonably settled.

'I'm going to have to go down to London for a while,' he told his mother that afternoon.

'Whatever you say son. We're both fine here. You've been wonderful on all this.'

He held her hand.

'I'll try and get back in a week.' He looked across at Trevor. 'Liverpool will duff your lot on Saturday,' he remarked.

He had discovered that Trevor was a Manchester United fanatic. He could name all the players, remembered the results, knew the league tables.

Trevor gurgled and smiled. 'Three-w-w-one, w-we'll w-win.'

They both laughed.

He drove down to London that night. To carry out his plan he needed to get back into Henson's house. He thought about telephoning Palmer, then decided to do it his way. It was three in the morning when he shoved open the back gate in Kensington. The key was still underneath the flowerpot, the patio door opened as before. He just hoped nothing inside had been removed.

The same musty odour filled the air. Quietly he tip-toed around removing the items he wanted. They weren't important now, Henson had no family, not even distant cousins. He'd been an adopted child and Casper was his best friend. Once he'd got what he came for, he left quickly, this time taking the key with him.

Next morning, from a call box, he rang Caroline Di Angello. When she answered, he put the phone down. Ten minutes later he was pressing on the door intercom of her Bloomsbury apartment.

'Caroline, it's Casper. Can I see you for a few minutes,' he said.

'Bloody hell!!' he heard her say. The buzzer sounded and the door opened.

'I hoped I might not have the pleasure again,' she said, when he reached her front door. 'What made you grow that ridiculous beard?'

'Well it's nice to see you too,' he replied.

It must have been nearly ten months since she'd stormed out of Ebury Terrace. Her hair was streaked a little lighter, a turtle neck blue and white top and shiny, pale blue slacks caused him to fantasise about what was underneath. Then she opened her mouth and spoiled the illusion.

'Casper, I said it to the police, I said it to your publishers and I said it to Henson, you're a louse.'

He smiled, 'Why's that?'

'Because you walked out on us.'

She turned her back on him and stalked off towards the living room. He shut the door and followed her down the passageway. The garish brightness of the large room made him blink. When he got close, she turned and gave him one of her eyeball stares. Her face looked like honey and cream and he could feel himself becoming aroused.

'Well I'm afraid it was necessary,' he said. 'It was a family problem. Nothing to do with any of you lot. Anyway, it was Henson I came to see you about.'

'You'd better sit down,' she said, dropping into an armchair. She lit up a cigarette. He picked a chair on the other side of the room.

'You look well,' he said.

'Huh. Flattery was never one of your more practised traits. What the bloody hell do you want?'

He coughed. He'd become unused to her distasteful cigarettes.

'The police still haven't released Henson's body. I want to put some pressure on them. Arrange for him to have a proper funeral. He's got no family, I'll have to sort it out.'

'Well if you'd been around, perhaps it wouldn't have happened.'

'What's that supposed to mean?'

'You were his friend.'

'Yes, but he was his own man as well. He had his peccadilloes. You know that as well as me. I wasn't his godfather. He'd never listen to me anyway.'

She crossed and uncrossed her legs and sucked on the cigarette.

'But he was your mentor. He got the best out of you. And he got the best for you. While you were in your ivory tower, writing your books, he did the wheeling and dealing. You wouldn't have made half so much money without him.'

Casper sighed. 'That's why I want to do what I can for him now. It's not right to say it was my fault. What basis have you got for saying that.' He glared at her.

'Because you're a louse, as I said.' She angrily stubbed out the half finished cigarette in an ashtray.

Casper got up and walked around the room, then stood with his back to her, looking out the window.

'Oh come on Caroline. I know we've had our ups and downs, but we did have some good times. Our relationship had burnt out, you know that. That doesn't make me a louse as far as Henson's death is concerned. There's got to be more to it than we know. Just try and help me to find out, that's all I'm asking.'

She lit up another cigarette. He stayed with his back to her, by the window. She spoke again.

'He was involved in drugs and things. Anything goes in that scene.'

'H'm, yes.' He turned to face her. She looked fidgety and puffed excessively on the cigarette.

'We were all supposed to be going to make that film together,' she said.

He ran his hand through his hair and moved closer towards her.

'I'd talked that through with him before I went away. We both agreed 'Flame in the Sky' wasn't suitable for a film. And that American consortium would have carved us up anyway. The figures didn't stack up. When I looked at the projections they were creaming off all the profit. It wasn't a viable return, not for me anyway.'

She puffed repeatedly on her cigarette and persistently flicked the ash into the ashtray.

'Well you still left us both in the lurch. It was a miserable thing to do.'

'I know it must seem like that, but as I said I had family problems. My mother's got cancer. She's in her eighties.'

For a moment neither of them said anything.

'You could have told us that.'

'I suppose I could. But that sort of thing's private.'

'We were your friends.'

'I know. Perhaps I was wrong.'

He was standing near her now. Desire was welling up in his body.

'The last thing Henson said to me,' he began, 'was about putting some money into a European film. You don't know anything about that do you?'

The expression on her face changed. He knew she was concealing something, there was more. He'd come to know her well enough to recognise when she was covering up. Many times in the past he'd seen that expression.

'Come on Caroline,' he said. 'This is important. Henson was a pal to us both. I've got to try and sort his things out. They're not going to release his body until they've made some progress on his murder. There's got to be a line on it somewhere and the police are bloody hopeless.'

She stubbed out her cigarette. She'd only smoked about half of it again.

'You're such a bastard. I don't know why I should tell you anything.' She got up from her chair, she was standing in front of him.

He looked at her in the way he used to look at her when he wanted her. It seemed to work. She ran her hand through her hair, turned her head to one side, pushed out her chest, turned her head back to face him and switched on the eyes.

He grabbed her around the waist and pulled her into his arms. She didn't resist. Then his hands and lips were everywhere. He dragged her to the floor, unzipped her slacks, lifted her top. There was no bra, everything was as he remembered. They mated, like two express trains on a collision course.

Lying in his arms afterwards, on the floor, she began to talk.

'Henson met up with my management people,' she said, while he stroked her hair and kissed her forehead. 'He thought the projections for my film looked good. From what little I know, he put your name to it as well, but that's as far as it went. We're on hold at the moment, because of lack of funding. That seems to be the way now unless Hollywood's involved.'

Soon afterwards he left. Making love to her he had felt nothing. It was a task, to get what he wanted. He knew that before he went there. The woman was so damn vain. He had to admit though, she was still a pretty good lay.

'I want to sort out a proper funeral for my friend,' Casper said. He was on the phone to John Palmer.

'We're still not in a position to release the body,' Palmer replied.

'Well what the bloody hell's happening?'

'Until we have a suspect, it's not possible.'

'I just hope it never happens to you. What about my missing money then? What have you come up with on that?'

'There's one or two leads we're working on.'

Casper could hear Palmer breathing heavily.

'One or two leads. Hell's bells man you sound like British Rail. My friend has been murdered, in my apartment. And there's the best part of half a million pounds of my money gone missing. And all you can say is there's one or two leads. It's been weeks now. If you don't mind me asking, just what have you achieved. If I don't get any sensible answers I'm going to my MP.'

'Mister Watkins, our enquiries are continuing. You can go to your MP if you like, but I must remind you that you are still on suspended bail. You haven't been completely eliminated from our enquiries.'

'Look Palmer, I've got to make some inroads on this. My solicitor suggests I instruct a private detective to try and find my money. I'm running short of cash. Can you tell me if there was anything at Henson's house to suggest he could have been bribed? I mean, everybody knows he was an old queer who smoked pot. Is there anything you can tell me on that? It's important to me. I repeat, I've got to do something about my money.'

There was silence at the other end, so Casper continued.

'Palmer, I'm sure my solicitor could get a court order.'

There was another long pause. This time Casper said nothing.

'There was a large quantity of drugs at the house,' Palmer said eventually.

'How large?' Casper enquired.

'Quite a lot.'

'How much is quite a lot? Was it hard drugs, soft drugs or what? Come on man, I need to know.'

'Hard drugs.'

'Heroin?'

'Yes, heroin and cocaine.'

'What sort of value?'

He heard Palmer breathing heavily again.

'I'm not at liberty to say.'

'Around twenty thousand pounds?' Casper asked.

'Probably, about that.'

'Rum and coke please. Have you any Mount Gay?' Casper asked. He was in the 'Dylan', striped vest was wearing blue and yellow that day.

'Should have. There used to be a bottle here somewhere,' the bar man said, then delved beneath the counter. It was just after eleven in the morning. There was only Casper and two other men in the bar.

'Here we are, not much left,' striped vest said, holding up an almost empty bottle of rum. Casper nodded. The barman poured a slug into a tall glass, threw in some ice, then snapped open the top of a coke, before placing it on the counter. Casper added some coke, took a sip and smacked his lips.

'The big guy Raul, I met in here last week, said he might be interested in some pieces I wanted to sell. He told me you'd know how to contact him.'

'He should be in around lunchtime,' striped vest said.

'Can't stay until then. Have you a number?'

When striped vest went to the till with Casper's money, he fumbled around the side and found a piece paper on which there was a list of telephone numbers. He wrote one on a till slip and handed it to Casper with his change.

'Shall I tell him who asked?' striped vest said.

'John Watkins,' Casper said, knocked back his drink and left. At Ebury Terrace, he checked the number with the list he'd made from Henson's blotter. It was there all right, repeated several times. A tick and cross were registered against it, which meant he'd tried and failed to get a reply.

On the off chance, he tried again.

'Yes,' a deep voice replied.

'Raul?' Casper asked.

'That's right.'

'We met in the 'Dylan' the other week. I said I may have some bits and pieces to sell. Do you remember?'

'Not really. It doesn't matter though. What have you got?'

'Oh, just a few nick knacks. Bits of silver, a few ornaments, nothing really expensive. Just taking up space.'

'Can you bring them to the 'Dylan'?' Raul said.

'I'd rather not. The silver pieces are a bit showy. You never know nowadays.'

'OK,' Raul said.

'What if I bring them to your place?'

For a second Raul made no reply, then said;

'Tell you what, there's a second-hand shop, 'Bring and Buy', it's called. About fifty yards from the 'Dylan'. The owner there helps me store things. I'll meet you there if you like.'

'Fine,' Casper said. 'I'll ring you when I've got everything together then.'

'OK,' Raul replied.

'I don't know your name? Only heard people call you Raul.'

'Kingdom. Raul Kingdom. And yours? We met at the 'Dylan', you say?'

'Yes, that's right. The other week. The name's Watkins, John Watkins. See you soon then.'

All the time they had been speaking, the bronze figurine was alongside Casper on the desk.

That same afternoon Casper was looking down into the eyes of a dazzling blonde, with shoulder length hair and thick red lipstick. She was sitting behind the reception desk in a fourth floor office, off Pimlico Road, and had been tapping at a keyboard. He was in the offices of Marchant, Dawes and Pembury, Management Consultants. Behind her, venetian blinds allowed shafts of bright sunlight to highlight the edges of her hair.

'Could I speak to someone about a venture trust involving B and R Enterprises,' Casper said.

'Do you have an appointment?' the blonde said, fluttering her eyelashes.

'No, but I could get a court order if it's required.'

For a moment a look of insolence flashed across her face. Then, like a kitten being disturbed in the middle of her afternoon snooze, she rose out of her chair and slinked, with long, gangly legs towards a door. Three quarters of the way there, she stopped and looked back at him over her shoulder.

'Your name sir, please?'

'Watkins, Casper Watkins.' He thought she had a wonderful pert behind. The blonde hair hung to a V just above it.

She smiled at him. 'Would you take a seat,' she said and went out through the door.

It must have been a good five minutes before she reappeared with a young man who she introduced as Nigel. In his late twenties, he was tall and dark, with a pointed nose, wearing a red and white striped shirt, with wide blue braces and dark blue trousers.

'If you could follow me please Mister Watkins,' he said and led the way down a passage to a glass walled room that was hot and very stuffy. He beckoned to an uncomfortable looking plastic chair.

'Now, how can I help?' he said.

'I'm looking for my money,' Casper said. Nigel half smiled and sidled uncomfortably into a similar chair opposite. Then he began to twiddle with a biro in his right hand.

'Are we supposed to have it?'

'I'm told you might. I'm a writer. They tell me I'm famous. My agent, Henson Littlewood, he's dead now, withdrew about half a million pounds from my bank account a few months ago. My enquiries indicate its whereabouts might be here, in a venture trust for B & R Enterprises.'

Nigel gave him a questioning stare, which changed into a half smirk.

'You're saying this man, your agent, Henson...'

'Littlewood,' Casper interrupted.

'Littlewood,' Nigel repeated, 'had authority to draw this amount of money from your bank account.'

'That's right. He had a mandate to do so.'

Nigel twiddled the biro some more. The smirk became a smile.

'So he withdrew the money. Now he's dead and you say it's in a venture account here, for B & R Enterprises?' He emphasised each sentence pointedly with the biro.

'At the risk of repeating myself, yes. Do you act for B and R Enterprises?'

'We do,' Nigel said awkwardly and shuffled uncomfortably in his seat. He had hazel eyes and very bushy eyebrows that curled up at the ends.

'Well then, can you tell me if you have the money?' Casper said.

'I'd have to check the paperwork. Was it invested in your name? I mean did you sign any of the forms?'

'No, I was away at the time.'

'Could you get copies of the cheques?'

'My bank tell me it was drawn in cash.'

A frown formed on Nigel's forehead.

'H'm,' he said and sighed. 'Well Mister Watkins that puts me in a difficult position. If you didn't sign the paperwork, it's unlikely the account would be in your name. You see for a venture trust there are certain tax forms to sign. If it's not in your name, by law, there's not much I can tell you about it.'

'What if it's in my Agents name?'

'Well if he's dead, it would form part his estate. Did he leave a Will?'

'Don't know. Shouldn't think so.'

'If that was the case we would have to wait for Letters of Administration.'

'Bloody hell man, if it's here, it's my money. Old Henson never had that sort of money. His signature is on the withdrawal forms at the bank. I can get copies.'

Nigel squirmed again in his seat and continued to twist the biro in his hand.

'But that wouldn't prove it was your money he invested. It might have been other money, do you see what I mean?'

'No, I don't see what you mean.' Casper sighed. 'Henson Littlewood drew five separate amounts of one hundred thousand pounds from my bank account on these dates.' Casper handed him a piece of paper on which the dates were written. 'If you've received those amounts around those dates, it's my money. Now, do you see what I mean?'

'H'm. Well maybe that's so, but it still doesn't give me the authority to release the information.'

'Bloody hell. You people are all the same. I just want to know where my money is. If I've got to go through the courts I will. Surely it would be simpler if you just told me if it's here.'

They stared at each other. Nigel twisted the biro more, now in both hands.

'I'll have to speak to Mister Marchant. He's not in the office today. Have you a phone number?'

Casper left, threatening his solicitor and the fraud squad. On his way out he slammed the door. The draft caused the venetian blinds behind the blonde to sway.

At Ebury Terrace there was a message on his answer phone from the nursing home. His mother hadn't been well. 'A bit of a turn. Probably reaction to the move,' they'd said.

'I'll drive up straight away,' he told them.

Within an hour the Ferrari's engines were roaring up the M6. Heavy rain swept across the motorway. The wipers flick-flacked to a constant beat. Stravinski, on a tape, kept him alert. He hadn't seen Jenny for days.

Meanwhile, she'd received a letter from Knott and Pearson stating they no longer required her services. It went on to say, she would be paid a months notice, but they asked her not to return. Several times she'd tried Casper's number, to no avail. Alone in her flat she was beginning to get desperate. Then the phone rang.

'Hi, it's me. Sorry I haven't been in touch,' Casper said. He was speaking on his mobile, a recent purchase, from somewhere along the M6; the reception was poor.

'Casper where are you?'

'Just north of Stafford. My mother's not too good. I've been in London, but I'm needed back at Mold.'

The line crackled. He went out of range.

'Hello, hello. Casper can you hear me?' she said.

Interference again intervened.

'Casper I can't hear you, you've gone out of range.'

She hung on just long enough for him to say, 'I'll ring you from the cottage'. Then he was gone.

Knott and Pearson's letter was on the table in front of her. At that moment the realities of her predicament caught up. She was a single girl, pregnant and living alone in London, with a mortgage to pay and no job. The father of her unborn child was a philanderer, who'd done a runner before when life got difficult. How could she be sure it would be different this time? The makings of a panic attack were beginning to set in.

While she totted up the debits on her mental balance sheet, her body began to shake. With Casper's cheque and the months notice money from Knott & Pearson, about another six weeks of survival was possible. Then she'd be destitute, unemployed, unmarried and a single mother. In other words, the bottom of the pit.

Her eyes misted, her chest tightened, her breathing laboured, her palms sweated, her feet felt numb. The room was closing in, she felt close to collapse. 'Somebody help me,' she screamed.

But nobody did. Desperation raced through her body like an infectious disease.

She got up, walked round, then sat down again. Tried lying on the bed; lying on the floor; sitting on the toilet. She gulped water, gobbled on an apple, turned on the radio, but nothing helped. For about two hours she sat in a chair by her window, rubbing her legs, looking out at nothing in particular. In her mind the reality of her fate slowly drowned out every other emotion. The walls around her were closing in. She had to get out of that flat.

Walking the streets, she bumped into people, tripped over pavements, lost her way. Like a demented animal on a busy road, she darted this way and that, unable to focus, concentrate, or take anything in. It was dark when she got back to the flat. She was exhausted and mentally drained. Again she tried the Mold number, again there was no reply. She didn't know his mobile, so she stumbled into bed. It was a long time before she fell into a sleep she hoped would last forever.

Casper was at the nursing home. His mother was very ill. She'd gone into a coma. He stayed the night. In the morning, briefly, he visited the cottage, to wash, shave and grab some breakfast, then went back to the nursing home. By lunchtime there'd been some improvement. She was awake, but weak. Most of the day he sat with her, holding her hand, talking slowly. Trevor flitted in and out, mumbling his concerns.

Casper had taken his lap-top with him. When his mother dozed, he sat in the corner at a small table and wrote. For two and a half days he hardly slept. The staff fussed in and out, asking if he wanted food or drink, but he brushed them away with an agitated wave of his arm. In those unlikely surroundings, with his mother ailing only feet away, he punched ferociously at the keys of his lap-top. Whenever she awoke, or when Trevor appeared, he would pause and spend time with them. Afterwards he would write and write, as though his life depended on it, until the story was done. And that's how he completed the tale of 'Catrin of Preseli'.

On the third day his mother rallied. She began to sit up; developed an appetite; became almost her old self. 'A mini stroke,' the doctor said. 'It often happens with people of her age. She is through the worst,' he added. So that night Casper returned to the cottage.

For most of those days Jenny lay on her bed, shaking, crying, moaning. Time and time again she tried phoning Casper, but in the end she gave up. She didn't go out, hardly ate. Tea and cream crackers became her diet until they ran out. Then she lay on the divan and sobbed.

By the third day, there were no more tears left to cry. Nothing mattered or was relevant anymore. Her life had become a void.

Desperate to try and get her mind on anything but her own despair, she switched on the television. The programmes were useless; people talking about broken love affairs, unfaithful husbands and battered wives. The only thing for it was to switch on that damn computer. All week it had cluttered her table and got in the way of everything she tried to do. She switched it on, more in anger than any sense of purpose.

'There's an e-mail for you,' a stupid message flashed.

'Outlook Express' was a function she'd found difficult from the outset. At last though, there was something for her brain to concentrate on.

The message rolled out on the screen. Blurred from crying, her eyes needed several attempts to take it all in.

'My dearest Jenny.

Well that's it, finished, I've downloaded the final pages tonight. At the moment it's something I'm proud of. See what you think. If you could check it through and print it out as usual that should do us.

Mother's better. A mini stroke I fear, but she's on the mend. No immediate handicaps, so far anyway. Just in case I'll have to stay on here for a while.

These last few days I've missed you very badly. Missed your pretty face, missed your smile, most of all missed your company. Being apart like this I realise now how much I love you. Just sorry at the moment I can't say it to you in person.

Coming back to the book, I'm thrilled with the way it's turned out. It's cleared a lot of clutter from the corners of my mind. I haven't actually got a title yet. 'Catrin of Preseli' is an idea. What do you think? Anyway we'll discuss it when we get together. It's as much your project as mine. Without your inspiration it wouldn't have been possible. You've been my guiding light from the start. I'm going to dedicate it to you, and we'll share any royalties. Perhaps we'll auction it as I suggested. That'll make the buggers at your place sweat.

By the way I have a lead on my money. Once again I've got you to thank for that. It looks like it may be invested in that film with Caroline Di Angello. If it makes any profit, we'll share that as well. Without your endeavours I wouldn't have got very far on that either.

All for now. Will telephone later in the week.

Love. Casper.'

Transfixed, she re-read it over and over, letting every word sink in. She must have re-read it twenty times or more and with each reading the hell in her body subsided. Just to convince herself it was all for real, she printed off a couple of copies.

CHAPTER

IT WAS THE FOLLOWING WEEK BEFORE CASPER WAS BACK IN LONDON. During that time he and Jenny didn't speak on the phone. Either he was at the nursing home, or Jenny was out. Communication had been via e-mail, mostly about the book. Some of her confidence had returned. She'd signed on at the social security and made an appointment with the Job Centre. She still hadn't told anybody about the pregnancy, or her parents about anything. One evening there'd been a message from Casper saying he would be down in a few days and would be in touch. 'We'll go out to dinner, somewhere nice, to celebrate the book.' The message had said.

'I'm expecting to meet Raul Kingdom here,' Casper said. He was at Hammersmith, in 'Bring and Buy', confronting Jenny's Pakistani man. His white baseball cap was pulled well down over his forehead and he was carrying a holdall which clanked with its contents each time he moved.

'Have you something to sell?' the man said to Casper and drew deeply on a cigarette.

'Yes, just a few bits and pieces. Family heirlooms mostly. Not worth much. Just taking up space.'

'Want me to take a look?'

'Better wait till Raul arrives. Trade busy?'

'Not particularly.' The man drew again on his cigarette. They talked a bit more about the world in general, while Casper browsed. He was inspecting a vase when he heard a deep voice behind him.

'Sorry I'm late.'

It was Raul, wearing a riotous shirt of reds, golds and lots of yellow, over a pair of cream slacks; Casper noticed the bulging muscles on his arms.

'We nearly did a deal without you,' Casper said.

Raul's big eyes floated back and fore between him and the other man.

'Malin wouldn't do that, would you my friend?' he guffawed. Huge pearly white teeth flashed. Malin shook his head nervously.

'I've got the pieces we talked about,' Casper said, lifting up the holdall. 'Shall I empty them here.' He pointed to a table.

'Yes, that'll do.' Malin said.

'Don't think they're worth much. Anyway, see what you think.' Very slowly Casper picked each piece out of the holdall, taking care to lay each one delicately on the table. Raul's huge presence was close up behind. He could hear his heavy breathing.

To begin with there were a few old vases which he'd brought from his apartment. While he'd been in Mold, one day, there had been a street market, and with this meeting in mind he'd bought a few bits of junk, to fill out the holdall.

'As I said, I don't expect they're worth much,' he said once he'd laid six or seven items on the table. Then his hands reached inside the bag for the silver. These were pieces he'd picked up from Henson's house, when he'd revisited. The miniature silver eagle Jenny had noticed was amongst them. It had been Casper's present for Henson, on his fortieth birthday. At the time it had cost him five hundred pounds.

He looked up and watched Raul's body stiffen. The big man blinked. 'Where did you get this?' he asked, handling it tentatively.

'Oh, in the family locker,' Casper said.

Raul's face was studded with concentration. Tenderly his big hands caressed the eagle.

Casper continued to extract more pieces he'd acquired from Henson's house. Malin moved in closer, picked up another one of the pieces and turned it over and over in his hands.